A KILLER TO HIS DYING BREATH

Bud Mann dropped to his knees, clutching at his stomach wound with one hand and with the other picking up the revolver he had dropped when he was hit, apparently determined to take Vint Lonegan with him to the grave. Grimacing with pain, Mann thumbed back the hammer and attempted to line up the barrel on Lonegan.

"Captain!" shouted the Frenchman, ready to shoot.

Lonegan waved his free hand at Beaumont as a signal not to fire. Holding his own gun leveled on Mann's chest, he barked, "Don't try it, Mann! If you do, I'll have to kill you!"

Bud Mann's eyes were venomous as he grunted heatedly, "Who cares? I'm gonna die anyway . . . but not before I kill you, Lonegan. It'll be the last thing I do, but I'm gonna kill you."

Lonegan's Colt .45 roared . . .

The Stagecoach Series
Ask your bookseller for the books you have missed

STAGECOACH STATION 46:

NORTH PLATTE

Hank Mitchum

Created by the producers of
**Wagons West, White Indian,
The Badge, and Abilene.**

Book Creations Inc., Canaan, NY · Lyle Kenyon Engel, Founder

BANTAM BOOKS

NEW YORK · TORONTO · LONDON · SYDNEY · AUCKLAND

NORTH PLATTE

A Bantam Book / published by arrangement with
Book Creations, Inc.
Bantam edition / March 1990

Produced by Book Creations, Inc.
Lyle Kenyon Engel, Founder

ISBN 0-553-28492-4

Published simultaneously in the United States and Canada

Bantam Books are published by Bantam Books, a division of
Bantam Doubleday Dell Publishing Group, Inc. Its trademark,
consisting of the words "Bantam Books" and the portrayal of
a rooster, is Registered in U.S. Patent and Trademark Office
and in other countries. Marca Registrada. Bantam Books,
666 Fifth Avenue, New York, New York 10103.

PRINTED IN THE UNITED STATES OF AMERICA

KR   0 9 8 7 6 5 4 3 2 1

STAGECOACH STATION 46:

NORTH PLATTE

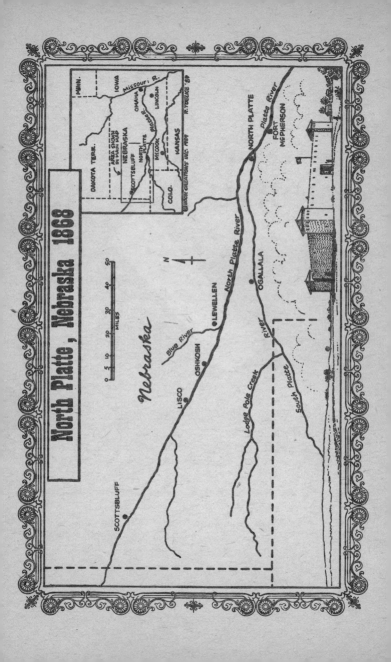

Chapter One

The warm evening wind gusted over the prairie, and a fat tumbleweed bounced across the dusty road in front of the six-horse team that pulled the stagecoach northward. Up in the box, the driver and his shotgunner clamped their hats on their heads as they twisted around on the seat, each leaning down on his side and looking in the open windows of the coach.

"We just crossed the Kansas-Nebraska border, folks!" the driver called. "Only fourteen miles to McCook, where we'll all get some rest!"

"Yeah!" the shotgunner shouted, adding, "Not to mention a hot meal!"

The passengers inside the coach all exchanged relieved glances.

Dabbing at her pretty face with a handkerchief, sixteen-year-old Patty Moore turned to her older sister and sighed, "I'll be glad for that. It seems all we've eaten for days has been dust. I declare, it's going to be the death of me."

"I think you had better get used to it," advised Becky Sue Moore with a giggle as she brushed back a stray lock of her long hair, which was as blond as her sister's was black. "There's going to be a lot more dust before we get to Scottsbluff."

1

Opposite the comely Moore sisters sat two elderly gentlemen, Roscoe Mulvey and Chester Adams, as well as a strikingly handsome young man named William Louis Beaumont. Adams gazed at each of the girls and asked, "Did I hear you young ladies say you were going to a wedding there?"

"Yes, sir, you did," replied eighteen-year-old Becky Sue with a smile. "We're from Grigston, Kansas—which isn't far from where we boarded the stage yesterday—and a very dear friend of ours from Grigston is getting married. As you gentlemen can probably tell, this is my sister's first experience on a stagecoach."

Patty gave her sister a petulant frown.

Becky Sue grinned at her and said, "But our friend is worth all this dust and discomfort, isn't she, Patty?"

"Of course," replied Patty, although her tone lacked the conviction of her words.

Patty turned and looked out the window at the sunset, and Becky Sue's dark-blue eyes focused on William Louis Beaumont, seated directly opposite her. During the one hundred miles the stage had traveled since she and her sister had boarded, the lovely young blonde had become infatuated with Beaumont.

By boldly asking pointed questions, Becky Sue had learned within the first twenty miles of the trip that Beaumont was a full-blooded Frenchman, born and raised in New Orleans—whenever he spoke, his slow Louisiana drawl sent chills down her spine—and that he was unmarried and twenty-eight years old. The tall and lean young Frenchman had a thin mustache and curly black hair with eyes to match, and his ready smile and quick wit made him extremely attractive to Becky Sue. Indeed, she thought him the kind of man she had long hoped would cross her path and one day become her husband.

He was elegantly dressed in a black pinstripe suit with vest and gold watch chain, and he wore a bone-white Stetson and shiny black boots. Becky Sue was fascinated by the pair of pearl-handled Colt .45s that Beaumont wore slung low on his slender hips, and she was certain that though he was smooth-talking and suave, he was no doubt tougher than he looked. The ten years difference in their ages was no point of discouragement to the Kansas beauty, for she had always been attracted to older men. And this particular older man enchanted her.

The Frenchman obviously felt Becky Sue's eyes on him and met her gaze, flashing her a pearly smile.

Her voice warm, the girl remarked, "You haven't told us why you are making this trip to Nebraska all the way from New Orleans, Mr. Beaumont."

"Business, Miss Moore," he answered quietly, exciting her unknowingly with his drawl.

Becky Sue waited for elaboration, but it did not come. Not wanting to pry, she turned the conversation to herself, hoping he would be interested in some of the things about her past that she counted as important.

While the pretty blonde prattled on, the stagecoach rolled northward and the sun sank below the western horizon, giving way to the purple twilight. Soon, except for the vague light cast by the stage's sidelamps, darkness prevailed over the flat, wind-swept prairie under the moonless, star-studded sky.

As the stagecoach drew near McCook, the passengers could see the rectangles of yellow light that marked the houses of the town, and above the wind two dogs could be heard barking at each other. The stage reached the edge of town, and the lamps illuminated a weathered sign clinging tentatively to a leaning post by a single nail and rattling in the wind. The sign welcomed the travelers to McCook, while at the same time advising them that the population was eight hundred and forty-one.

William Louis Beaumont perked up at the tinkling sound of a barroom piano as the coach rolled down the dusty street. Leaning forward in the seat, he looked through the window as they passed the Broken Lance Saloon.

The coach ground to a halt at the stage office, and the crew climbed down from the box. While the shotgunner removed the passengers' overnight cases from the boot, the driver opened the door, assisting the travelers out. Beaumont alighted from the coach after the two elderly men, then turned and offered his hand first to Patty and then to Becky Sue, who gave the Frenchman a dazzling smile of appreciation.

When all the passengers had disembarked, the driver reminded them that they would be leaving at six-thirty in the morning for the seventy-mile jaunt to North Platte. "Be here on time, or we leave without you," he cautioned.

Looking across the street at the Great Plains Hotel, Roscoe Mulvey sighed and said, "These old bones are tired. I'm heading for bed right now."

"Me, too," agreed Chester Adams.

Becky Sue looked up at the handsome Frenchman and asked, "Are you going to the hotel now, Mr. Beaumont?"

Shaking his head while brushing the dust from his suit, Beaumont replied, "No, I'm going over to that saloon. Perhaps a snort or two of whiskey will remove this awful dust from my throat—if not from my clothes."

The pretty blonde giggled appreciatively at his witticism. Batting her eyelashes coquettishly, she said softly, "Well, good night, then. I'll see you in the morning."

Bidding his fellow passengers good night, the Frenchman then headed for the Broken Lance. As he drew near, two cowboys staggered through the bat-wings and crossed the boardwalk to their horses, where their advanced state of inebriation made mounting the animals difficult. Beaumont smiled, adjusted the gun belt on his slender waist, and pushed through the swinging doors. The piano was playing loudly, but the even louder, off-key voice of a drunken trail hand trying to sing the words to the tune almost obliterated the music, as did the ring of hollow laughter that seemed to haunt this saloon like every other.

Beaumont assessed the large, smoky room as he walked toward the bar. In the far corner a small, thin man was playing the piano, while toward the back a number of card games were active. A heavily painted redhead brushed by the tall, handsome Southerner, giving him an approving appraisal, and he flashed her a smile and politely touched his hat brim without breaking his stride. Reaching the bar, he put a black-booted foot to the rail and pushed back his hat, waiting for the bartender.

Coming over to his new patron, the bartender wiped the mahogany bar in front of Beaumont and asked, "What'll it be?"

"Whiskey," drawled Beaumont to the short, balding man whose broad face was framed by a pair of bushy, muttonchop sideburns. "Make it three fingers."

Nodding, the bartender placed a shot glass in front of his latest customer and queried while pouring, "What part of the South you from?"

"Louisiana," came the drawn-out answer. "A little river town called New Orleans."

"I've heard of it," the bartender quipped in return and then walked away to attend to another customer.

William Louis Beaumont picked up the glass of amber-colored liquid and turned around to survey the crowd through the cloud of smoke. Resting one elbow on the bar, he sipped the whiskey, peripherally aware that the redhead was across the room pointing him out to another bar girl. It did not surprise him, for his good looks and gentlemanly manners often drew attention from the ladies.

Beaumont's dark eyes scanned the room for several moments, but seeing no familiar face, he turned back to the bar. He was draining the contents of his glass when the piano's tinkling trailed off in the middle of a song, and looking into the mirror behind the bar, the Frenchman saw that the crowd was gathering around a table a few feet away. The hubbub diminished, and soon there was an expectant silence in the place. Even the pianist deserted his instrument and stepped close to the table that had become the center of attraction.

The poker players had been whittled down to two men who sat facing each other in a blue haze of cigar smoke. The men who had dropped out of the game, along with the other spectators who were pressing around the table, watched with hushed admiration the two men who were still playing with deadly seriousness. There was a virtual fortune in gold pieces and currency piled in the middle of the table.

One of the players was Bud Mann, and he looked every inch the professional gambler that he was. He wore an expensive gray suit, a ruffled white silk shirt, and a black flat-crowned hat over his dark hair, and each of his slender hands bore a flashy diamond ring on its little finger. There was a diamond stickpin in his black tie and a solid-gold watch chain dangling on his vest. His impassive gray eyes, deeply set in a face that looked as though it had been chipped from granite, gave away nothing—and also missed nothing—and his thin, colorless lips were clamped around a costly cigar.

From time to time Mann stole a furtive look at an accomplice standing just behind his opponent. The antithesis of his elegant boss, lean and hollow-cheeked Chick Palmer had a long shag of greasy hair hanging over his dirty, frayed shirt collar. There was evil lurking in his dark-brown eyes, and his hands moved restlessly as though he were impatient for Bud Mann to give him the signal to torture or kill for him.

The ruggedly handsome muscular man sitting opposite the gambler was leaning forward on his elbows, studying the cards in his hands. Vint Lonegan's lively pale-blue eyes were as warm as his opponent's were cold, and his mouth might have seemed too delicate in a softer face. The wide-brimmed hat he wore was tilted over his angular face and covered most of his neatly trimmed ash-blond hair. Not yet thirty-one, the tracery of lines on Lonegan's face was evidence of a hard-lived life. He had the look of the military about him, though he was dressed in civilian clothing.

There was not so much as a whisper in the crowd. Lonegan studied his cards for a long moment, then folded them into his palm and, stroking his mustache, said simply, "I'll keep these." Shoving a stack of gold pieces toward the huge pot in the center of the table, he looked across at Mann and added, "You'll have to match this to see my hand. So what'll it be? Are you in? If so, play what you've got, or deal yourself some more."

"I'm in—but I'm out of cash," Bud Mann responded, clearing his throat. "I'll have to put in an IOU."

Lonegan's pale blue eyes seemed to look right through the professional gambler. "Not acceptable," he rejoined coldly. "But that diamond on your left hand will do."

Mann's face flushed with sudden anger. "My word isn't good enough?"

Vint Lonegan's deep voice was more like a growl. "I can't spend your word," he replied, easing back in the chair. "Looks like the game ends here."

The gambler's lips twitched. He burned Lonegan's face with furious eyes as he pulled off the ring and piled it onto the pot.

"All right," Lonegan declared, nodding. "Now we can proceed." His accent betrayed him as a Northerner, for there was a touch of New England in it.

Reaching over for the deck, Mann discarded one card, then dealt himself one card from the deck, placing it in his hand. After another round of betting, for which

Mann used his diamond stickpin in lieu of cash, they were ready to show their hands.

Necks craned in the tightly packed crowd as the big, muscular Lonegan spread his cards faceup on the table. Eyeing them briefly, Bud Mann smiled slowly and victoriously. He fanned out his own cards for his opponent to see and then puffed rapidly on his cigar. A number of the onlookers gasped, and this was followed by a low murmur of voices.

"Looks like you lose," Mann remarked triumphantly, reaching for the pot to rake it toward himself while his cohort, standing behind Lonegan, chuckled and scratched his three-day growth of beard.

Suddenly Vint Lonegan snarled, "Not so fast," and he grabbed Mann's wrist, staying his hand. Regarding the gambler with piercing eyes, he said through gritted teeth, "It's usual for a deck to have *one* ace of clubs. I think we better check and see how many this one has."

The crowd tensed, and the murmuring died, replaced by utter silence.

Bud Mann's face went beet red. Taking the cigar out of his mouth, he stubbed it out angrily in the ashtray. "Are you calling me a cheat?"

"I don't have to if there's another ace of clubs in this deck," the big man said sardonically, his eyes narrowed.

Mann immediately clapped his right hand over the deck of cards.

"Take your hand off the deck," Lonegan warned.

"You're asking for trouble," warned the gambler. "If you examine the deck, I'll have to take it as an out and out accusation."

"Then let's call it that," agreed Lonegan icily. "Move your hand."

The bartender slid a few steps along the bar, then stopped, his hands dropping out of sight.

The gambler suddenly pulled his hand away, but he thrust it inside his coat. Lonegan's right hand was a blur as, in the blink of an eye, his Colt .45 was out of the holster with its hammer snapped back, leveled at the gambler's belly. "I wouldn't try it if I were you. This slug'll be in your guts far quicker than you can grab the gun you're obviously wearing in a shoulder holster."

People in the crowd elbowed and shoved each other as they hurriedly backed away, while sweat beads popped out on Mann's brow as his hand lowered slowly away from his coat. His eyes darted to Chick Palmer, who still stood directly behind Lonegan, and then he again focused on the big man's ice-blue glare.

Lonegan levelly announced, "Now, let's take a look at that deck." Then suddenly he stiffened.

The click of a hammer being cocked sounded unnaturally loud in the hushed saloon. In a voice as cold as the muzzle pressing into Vint Lonegan's neck, Chick Palmer warned, "Game's over. You lose."

Bud Mann's rigid face relaxed, and he declared slyly, "A fella who plays for high stakes needs to have a friend close by."

"You're right—and he's got one," a voice behind Palmer declared in a cool southern drawl. "And I'm holdin' a .45 caliber revolver against the back of this ugly dude's skull."

Chick Palmer tensed, but his hand holding the weapon on Lonegan did not relax.

"Now, mister," ordered William Louis Beaumont, "you just ease that weapon away from my friend's neck."

Bristling, Palmer retorted, "You want me to send your friend to the graveyard, Rebel?"

"If you do, you'll be right behind him," promised the Southerner. "And these nice people here will get all splattered with what little brains are inside your greasy head."

The crowd waited expectantly, looking from one man to the other as if trying to determine which one of them would back down.

"I ain't movin' the gun until your pal takes his gun off of *my* friend," Palmer said stubbornly.

Jaw squared, Vint Lonegan held firm.

"Well, now," said the gambler, forcing a smile. "Looks like we've got us a Mexican standoff here."

From the corner of his eye the Frenchman suddenly caught movement behind the bar. Whipping out his other revolver, Beaumont fired at the bartender, who was bringing his shotgun to bear on the Southerner. The bullet missed the bartender's head by inches, shattering the large mirror behind him. The balding man dropped the shotgun on the bar like it had suddenly turned red-hot, while both Mann and Palmer jerked at the roar of Beaumont's gun and the bar girls screamed.

Still holding the muzzle of the gun in his right hand against Palmer's skull, Beaumont pointed the smoking one at the bartender and warned slowly, "You try a thing like that again and the next one goes between your eyes. No doubt this fella's a good and regular customer, so you felt obliged to back him up . . . but a good customer's worthless to a dead man, wouldn't you agree?"

The bartender stood frozen in his tracks, owl-eyed.

"Now, reach down real slowlike and pick up the scattergun," commanded Beaumont.

Blinking fearfully, the bartender obeyed. When it was in his grasp, Beaumont instructed, "Break it open and empty out them shells, then leave it on the top of the bar and back away from it.

The trembling man complied.

Pressing the muzzle of his revolver harder against Palmer's head, Beaumont said, "Now, let's everybody relax 'cause this ugly fella is going to take his gun from my friend's neck."

"Over my dead body!" snapped Palmer.

"If that's your wish . . ." drawled the Southerner.

Palmer's body was beginning to shake. "I'll take your friend with me!" he screeched.

Raising his other .45, Beaumont pulled back the hammer, extended his arm, and lined the muzzle on the gambler's face. "I'm tired of this game, Mann. You tell your monkey to put down his weapon. I'm going to count to three. If he doesn't do it, I will pull both triggers at once. You won't feel my friend's bullet tear into your ever-loving guts, because you will already be dead." Widening his black eyes, the Frenchman added sternly, "I assure you, I am not bluffin'."

Both the gambler and his accomplice swallowed hard as Beaumont began, "One . . . two . . . th—"

"Put the gun down, Chick!" shouted Mann, sweat running into his eyes.

Palmer snarled and lowered the revolver. Easing the hammer into place, he let the weapon clatter to the floor.

Vint Lonegan stood up and stepped around the table to Bud Mann, still holding the cocked .45 in his right hand. Reaching inside the gambler's coat with his left, he slipped the small revolver from its holster and shoved it under his belt.

Mann glared at him with murder in his eyes.

Opening his palm, Lonegan ordered, "Now, let's have the derringer."

"Derringer?"

"Come on. I know you have one. Every gambler I've ever met carries a derringer."

Reluctantly, Mann pulled the object in question from a deep vest pocket and laid it in the big man's hand.

Lonegan turned around and looked at the Southerner, giving him a crooked smile. "Thanks, *amigo*."

Still holding the muzzle at the base of Chick Palmer's skull, Beaumont grinned. "You are quite welcome."

Vint Lonegan cocked his head and looked intently at the Southerner for a few moments, obviously trying to place him. Giving his head a brief, quick shake, he then slipped the derringer into a coat pocket and gestured to the redheaded bar girl who stood close by. "Would you come here, ma'am?"

Nervously, the heavily painted woman edged her way forward.

"I want you to help me for a moment," Lonegan explained casually.

She nodded silently with a weak smile.

Pointing to Bud Mann's "winning" cards still fanned faceup on the table, Lonegan asked, "Would you lift the ace of clubs out of that hand and show it to these nice people?"

Every eye in the place focused on the card as she displayed it to their view.

Nodding, he took the card from her fingers and then instructed her, "Now, would you pick up that deck of cards Mr. Mann dealt himself his winning hand from and see if there's an ace of clubs in there?"

Bud Mann suddenly licked his lips nervously, and dread was stamped visibly on his face as the redhead began sifting through the deck. Within seconds she produced the ace of clubs and again held it up for all to see.

"Well shut my mouth and call me Jefferson Davis!" exclaimed William Louis Beaumont, exaggerating his drawl. "That man sho' nuff is a dirty, slick-fingered cheat!"

Chick Palmer's face reddened with anger and he flinched, but he straightened his back when Beaumont shoved the muzzle hard against his head.

"I'll take your coat," Lonegan commanded the gambler.

"My coat?" echoed the man in bewilderment.

Regarding the man sardonically, Lonegan extended his free hand and explained, "I've got to have something to carry my winnings in."

Bud Mann stood up and slid out of his obviously expensive coat. Lonegan took it and dropped it on an adjacent table. Then, holstering his Colt .45, he spread the coat open and piled the gold and currency on it, laying aside the diamond ring and five twenty-dollar gold pieces. Rolling the coat up in a neat bundle, he tied the arms in a knot and, running his gaze over the circle of faces around him, said, "All you folks may leave now."

"What are you gonna do?" demanded Mann.

Ignoring the question, Lonegan asked, "You got any more cohorts in the place?"

"I'm not telling you a thing," the gambler replied sullenly.

"Your scummy pal will tell us," said Beaumont, pushing the muzzle hard against Chick Palmer's head once more.

"Oh, no, I won't!" blurted Palmer.

With his other revolver, the Frenchman fired a shot into a far wall. Again pressing the muzzle of the Colt in his right hand into Palmer's head, Beaumont threatened, "The next one goes in your cranium, sir. Tell my friend what he wants to know. Now!"

Some of the crowd had filed out, but several men were still inside the saloon. One of them spoke up, telling Lonegan, "Mann rode into town three days ago with five men—the same bunch he's had with him when he's visited McCook plenty of other times." He paused and looked around, then added, "Chick Palmer's the only one of the bunch in here, but I'm sure the others are still in town. They always seem to ride together."

While the gambler gave the man a furious look, Lonegan thanked him. He turned and left, and moments later the saloon was empty except for Vint Lonegan, William Louis Beaumont, Bud Mann, Chick Palmer, and the bartender.

Turning to the bartender, the big blond man said, "You've got kerosene around here somewhere to fill these lamps. Get it."

"K-kerosene?" gulped the bartender. "What for?"

"Just do it!" Lonegan snapped.

While the bartender hurried to a storeroom, Bud Mann looked at Lonegan with hatred and demanded, "You're not gonna burn the saloon down, are you?"

"Naw," Lonegan answered, grinning. "I'm gonna burn your boots."

The gambler's mouth fell open. "My boots? You can't burn my boots! They're expensive! Why, I paid—"

"Shut up!" rasped the big man. "I figure you boys are gonna have a desire to collect your four friends and follow me. I'd rather you didn't, because then I might have to kill you—so to discourage such a move, I'm gonna burn your boots. It'll take you a little time to get new ones, and I'd strongly suggest that during that time, you think it over carefully—'cause if I see you again, it'll just be more than I can stomach."

"You dirty rat!" Mann bawled, his face reflecting his fury. "I swear I'll find you! And when I do—"

"Like I said, you low-life cheater," cut in Lonegan, "I'll have to kill you if you come after me."

The bartender returned, carrying a can of kerosene. His brow was puckered and there was uneasiness in his eyes. To the big man, he said, "Please, don't burn down my place."

"I wouldn't think of it," replied Vint Lonegan. Turning to the Southerner, he asked, "By the way, what's your name, Rebel?"

Standing erectly while still holding the gun against Chick Palmer's head, the Southerner drawled, "William Louis Beaumont. From New Orleans. And you are . . . ?"

"Vint Lonegan. You can just call me Vint."

Bud Mann's mouth fell open again. Glancing back and forth between the two men, he gasped, "You mean you two don't even know each other?"

"We do now," Lonegan replied with amusement. His face then hardened, and he demanded, "You two take off your boots and socks."

Shaking his head in disbelief, the gambler swore under his breath but complied. His cohort started to complain, but Beaumont barked, "Do what the man told you!" Snarling angrily, Chick Palmer pulled off his boots.

Ordering the men to their feet, Vint Lonegan hustled them and the bartender into the storeroom, telling Mann and Palmer, "It sure irritates the dickens out of me for a two-bit gambler to cheat me in a card game. Makes me even more irritated to have a greasy gunslick put a muzzle to the back of my neck. You two ought to count your lucky stars that I'm not just some drifter. You'd have been dead by now if I was." So saying, he locked them inside.

"You're a dead man, Lonegan!" Bud Mann shouted through the closed door. "A dead man!"

With a shrug, Lonegan holstered his revolver, then walked back to the table and picked up the coat loaded with his winnings. Leaving several of the gold pieces on the table, explaining they were to pay for the shattered mirror and the kerosene, he picked up the two pairs of boots stuffed with socks in his other hand while the Southerner carried the kerosene, and then the two men hurried outside. Lonegan pulled Mann's derringer from his coat pocket, emptied it of its single cartridge, and then dropped it inside one of the boot. He did the same thing with the gambler's revolver and then Chick Palmer's gun. Pouring the flammable liquid inside and over the boots, Lonegan pulled out a matchbox and struck the match, and then lit the boots. With satisfaction, he stood watching them ignite. Then he turned to Beaumont and declared, "I'm much obliged for what you did, partner."

Beaumont smiled and remarked, "I just hate to see a man disadvantaged and outnumbered."

Extending the diamond ring to the Frenchman, Lonegan asked, "Think this'll fit you? I won it fair and square in a card game."

Grinning broadly, Beaumont slipped the sparkling ring on the little finger of his left hand. "You're truly a generous fellow, Vint Lonegan," he said to the big man. "Especially for a Yankee."

"It's just my nature to be benevolent," Lonegan responded, chuckling.

"I take it you're about to depart this fair town," said Beaumont.

"That's correct," Lonegan confirmed, picking up the bundle that contained his winnings. "I'm leaving as of this moment." He walked toward his horse, tethered to the hitch rail. There were two other horses tied there, both good ones, and the one that had a silver-trimmed saddle with matching bridle most certainly belonged to Bud Mann.

"Which way you headed?" queried Beaumont.

"North."

"Going anywhere near North Platte?"

"Quite close."

"I came in on the stage a little while ago," explained Beaumont, "the one that's headin' for North Platte in the morning. I'm tryin' to find a man, but I only know that he's supposed to be somewhere in the general vicinity of North Platte." He paused, then suggested, "Look here, I'll have to buy a horse in North Platte, anyway, so if I could get the hostler here in town to sell me a horse right now, would you mind if I ride with you? It'd just take me a few minutes to go retrieve my carpetbag from the stage line and change into more appropriate ridin' attire."

Lonegan shoved the coat into his saddlebag and buckled it, and then turned and grinned at the Southerner. "A man who just saved my hide is plenty welcome to ride with me," he replied warmly. "Only why bother the hostler when there's a good horse and saddle for sale right here?" He reached over and patted the gambler's bay. "This animal clearly belongs to Mann, but I hereby declare it and the tack for sale. I'd say they're worth about fifty dollars, wouldn't you?"

"Lonegan, I don't understand you," the Southerner responded, laughing. "After what Mann did to you, I'd say you have a right to just *take* his horse!"

"Now, Mr. Beaumont, that'd be an illegal thing for a government man to do."

"Government man?" echoed Beaumont in surprise. "Well, I knew you weren't just a shiftless drifter, but I didn't figure you for that. What kind of government man?"

"I'll explain later," replied Lonegan. "Right now, I'd like to get on the road." Reaching into his pocket, he pulled out the remaining gold pieces and counted out fifty dollars. Stuffing the money into Chick Palmer's saddlebag, he remarked, "They'll know what it's for. Let's go get your belongings and ride."

Chapter Two

Twenty minutes later, Vint Lonegan and William Louis Beaumont galloped northward out of McCook. After riding their horses hard for a while, they hauled up beside a small creek, which was visible in the vague light of the stars and the crescent moon that had finally risen, to let the horses rest and take their fill of water.

Watching his mount drink, Beaumont said to Lonegan, "Now, tell me about your job."

The fair-haired man replied, "I'm a captain in the U.S. Army. Did my part in the Civil War on the Union side, of course. I'm from Pawtucket, Rhode Island."

"Well, I knew for sure you weren't from Alabama," quipped Beaumont. "Why are you in civilian clothes instead of a uniform?"

"The nature of my job," Lonegan responded. "At the close of the war three years ago, General Grant asked me to remain in the Army and help track down men who had deserted the Union forces during the war. The government hasn't forgiven them for their desertion, so it's my job to find them, arrest them, and take them in for trial. Most of them have turned to outlawing since they deserted, and I've been running them down mainly in Colorado, Wyoming, Nebraska, and the Dakota Territories."

"Seems a mighty impressive job for a fella your age." He squinted through the gloom. "Just how old are you, anyway?"

"Thirty. Almost thirty-one."

"Tell me, whose trail are you on now?"

"A deserter who's selling repeater rifles to the Indians—and if the gunrunning isn't stopped, things are going to get out of hand with the hostiles. Most of the time the Army is badly outnumbered when they go into battle with them, and the only equalizer has been that the Indians have just had single-shot rifles while the Army's had repeaters. According to witnesses, the man I'm after passed through McCook going north only a few days ago. Just now I'm headed for Fort McPherson —which is about thirteen miles southeast of North Platte—to see if they've had any more word on him."

"How are the guns bein' smuggled in?" asked the Southerner.

"On wagon trains. The Army is inspecting as many of them as possible, but we're terribly shorthanded and we can't check them all."

"It's a big country out here," agreed Beaumont, nodding. "I can see why the task would be a tough one."

Changing the subject, Lonegan asked, "How about you, William? You mentioned that you're looking for a man. Does it have to do with your job?"

"No," Beaumont replied flatly. "Personal matter. I owe the man, and I want to find him so I can pay him." Then he smiled and added, "And call me Beau."

"Okay." Lonegan then cocked his head and assessed his companion quizzically. "Tell me something. Why did you step in to help me, knowing I'm a Northerner?"

Beaumont smiled slowly. "Well, I fought in the war, too—Confederate Army, as you no doubt would guess. I was a lieutenant when the war ended."

"A Rebel helping a Yankee?"

"I was wounded at the second battle of Bull Run,

and a Yankee officer saved my life. But I never got to thank him, so helpin' you was my way of payin' that Yankee officer back."

Lonegan took a deep breath and exclaimed, "Thank the good Lord for that Yankee officer!"

They both smiled and then were pensive for a few moments. Studying Lonegan's face, Beaumont finally inquired, "You married, Captain? Seems a woman would have a hard time bein' married to a travelin' man like you."

"Well, there's no one to have to put up with my work. I only met one woman who seriously interested me, but she's out of reach."

Beaumont nodded silently, assuming the woman must be married to someone else.

"How about you?" asked Lonegan. "You married?"

"No," came the ready answer. "Haven't met the perfect woman yet."

Lonegan suggested they ride again, and the two men mounted up. After riding another hour, they pulled into a shallow, grassy draw and agreed it was time to get some sleep. Dismounting, they began uncinching the saddles, and William Louis Beaumont commented how thoughtful it was that Bud Mann had provided him with a bedroll as well. The two men laid their bedrolls out on the ground, used their saddles for pillows, and stretched out, each pulling a blanket over himself. They dropped their hats over their faces and grew quiet.

After a few moments, Beaumont broke the silence. "Vint . . ."

"Yeah?"

"What does the Army do with these low-down deserters when you bring them in?"

"Washington has given me full authority to hang them. But to date none of the thirteen men I've brought in have been hanged."

"Oh? How come?"

"They came in draped over their saddles."

"Oh."

Silence settled around them for a few minutes and then Beaumont asked, "You think those fellas are gonna come after us?"

"Probably."

"Yeah. I think so, too."

Dawn was streaking the eastern horizon a rosy gray as five shadowed figures waited beside their horses and watched a sixth man hurrying toward them from the edge of the shallow draw. As he drew up, panting, he reported, "It's them all right, Bud, and they're sleepin' like babies."

Bud Mann grinned maliciously. "Pretty soon we'll put them to sleep permanently. Now, you and Shorty sneak in there downwind and get the horses, then lead 'em back here. I don't want a stray bullet hitting my horse."

"Will do," the outlaw assured the gambler.

The two men went to do Mann's bidding, and ten minutes later they returned with the two horses, affirming that both men were still asleep in their bedrolls with their hats over their faces.

"Good!" exclaimed the gambler. "Are they lying together?"

"Yeah," replied Burns.

"Okay," said Mann. "We'll go in and cover them from the front and sides." He sneered and then added, "I want those buzzards to wake up looking right at me and Chick—and don't any of you start shooting before I do. Me and Chick're going to have us a little fun before they die." He looked at his right-hand man, whose face expressed the delight he was obviously feeling at the notion of torturing the two men.

Bud Mann's face was eager with anticipation as he and his five men took their places at the crest of the draw. The dull light coming from the eastern horizon revealed the two covered figures lying peacefully, hats pulled low. Mann motioned at the other four to move in as he and Palmer tiptoed slowly down the gentle slope.

When each armed man was in place, Mann nodded and then cut the still air by shouting, "Hey, wake up, you two! We've got a little surprise for you!"

The sleeping forms did not move.

Repeating himself, Mann shouted louder. When there was still no motion under the blankets, he cursed the two men while stomping over to the form on his right and kicking it hard. The blanket sailed away, exposing a long, narrow pile of grass. The tilted hat flopped to the ground.

Chick Palmer railed vituperatively and kicked the other form. It, too, was a pile of grass.

Bud Mann's face twisted with rage. He opened his mouth, but before he could say anything more, a voice from behind him blared, "I told you not to come after me, Mann!"

The gambler's body whipped around. Standing on the eastern edge of the draw, silhouetted against the brightening sunrise, were Vint Lonegan and William Louis Beaumont. Both of the Frenchman's Colt .45s were cocked and leveled on the group, as was Lonegan's revolver.

Mann stood with his mouth open, speechless. His five men were likewise standing like statues, their weapons pointed toward the ground. Lonegan broke the silence by saying, "You work faster than I gave you credit for. I didn't think you could come up with boots and weapons so quickly, not to mention another horse." He paused a few seconds and then snapped, "Well, you needn't have bothered with the guns. Drop 'em!"

Bud Mann's loathing for Vint Lonegan had obviously pushed him beyond the point of reason, for instead of complying, he growled, "You took my guns once, Lonegan. I don't think I'm gonna let you do it again."

"You haven't got a chance," Lonegan warned him.

"Are you kidding? There's six of us and two of you!" Mann retorted. "You may get a couple of us, but you'll die for certain! Best thing for you to do is give me back my money and ride on."

"I'd hardly call it *your* money, you cheating snake in the grass!" bellowed the Army captain. "Now, do as I said and drop your gun—and tell your slimy friends to do the same."

Chick Palmer whispered from the side of his mouth, "I'm with you, Bud. If we hit the ground fast and do a roll, they're bound to miss us, and the six of us can take 'em."

Without warning, the gambler brought his gun up and fired. But the sharp report from his gun came a split second after that of Vint Lonegan's, who got off a shot first. While Mann's bullet missed his target by two feet, Lonegan's landed just where he had aimed—and the gambler staggered and clawed at the bleeding hole in his stomach. Immediately following his boss's lead, Chick Palmer was just as unsuccessful as he was cut down by one of Beaumont's revolvers.

Two other of Mann's cronies brought their guns up and began shooting, but Lonegan and Beaumont blasted away with deadly accuracy. One of the men took a slug through the head and blood splattered as he went down like a rotten fence post in a high wind. The other man got off two wild shots before a .45 slug exploded his heart. The last two gang members had been slower to bring their weapons into play. Finally both men swung their muzzles up, ready to fire, but they were cut down before they could do so, and they sprawled facedown in the dew-covered grass.

Bud Mann dropped to his knees, clutching at his stomach wound with one hand and with the other picking up the revolver he had dropped when he was hit, apparently determined to take Vint Lonegan with him to the grave. Grimacing with pain, Mann thumbed back the hammer and attempted to line up the barrel on Lonegan.

"Captain!" shouted the Frenchman, ready to shoot.

Lonegan waved his free hand at Beaumont as a signal not to fire. Holding his own gun leveled on Mann's chest, he barked, "Don't try it, Mann! If you do, I'll have to kill you!"

Bud Mann's eyes were venomous as he grunted heatedly, "Who cares? I'm gonna die anyway . . . but not before I kill you, Lonegan. It'll be the last thing I do, but I'm gonna kill you."

Lonegan's Colt .45 roared. The slug ripped into Mann's heart, its impact flattening him on his back. His reflex fired his gun into the air, but the gambler never heard its roar.

The entire shootout had taken less than half a minute. Lonegan and Beaumont descended the gentle slope and stood over the six dead men, and with the warmth of the rising sun on their backs, they began punching cartridges from their gun belts and reloading their weapons.

"Whew," sighed Beaumont, "I'm sure glad you decided we should fool those boys."

"I knew Mann would come—he was just a little faster at it than I thought he would be. I'm glad we followed our instincts."

The handsome Frenchman drawled, "Now, what are we goin' to do with all these corpses?"

"We sure can't bury them," Lonegan replied drily. "That is, unless you've got a shovel in your hip pocket."

Beaumont shrugged and said, "Why not just leave them here and let the coyotes and the other prairie varmints have a banquet?"

"I'd like to," admitted Lonegan, "but as an officer of the United States Army, I have to uphold a degree of dignity in affairs. No, I'm afraid we'll have to find their horses and haul their carcasses into the next town for proper burial."

Beaumont laughed. "You sure are somethin', Captain Lonegan. That cheatin' skunk was bent on killin' you, and yet you're goin' to see to it that he gets a dignified burial!"

Lonegan spread his hands. "Life has its ironies, my friend. Let's accept that fact and proceed accordingly." He looked around and then mused, "They couldn't have stashed their horses too far from here. Let's go find them."

Twenty minutes later, Captain Vint Lonegan and William Louis Beaumont rode north leading a string of six horses. By late morning, they had ridden into the wind-blown town of Maywood, Nebraska, and as they headed up the sunbleached street, the town's citizens paused to gawk at the gory procession of dead men draped over their horses' backs.

Lonegan pointed at the Maywood Cabinetry Shop and Funeral Parlor. "Let's deposit these fellas and then get us some breakfast," Lonegan suggested. "I think we've earned it."

"You won't get any argument from me," Beaumont snickered.

They drew up in front of the dilapidated building and Lonegan dismounted, saying, "You wait here. I'll be right back."

Sitting impatiently in his saddle, holding the lead rope, the man from New Orleans avoided the eyes of the townspeople who stood looking on and whispering. He hoped Lonegan would hurry. He did not like being a spectacle.

Several minutes passed. The horses bearing the lifeless bodies nickered and danced about nervously. Beaumont licked his lips and cast a wondering look toward the shadowed interior of the building where Lonegan had disappeared. What was taking him so long?

Just then a short, skinny man emerged from the

marshal's office across the street and beelined toward him. The little man was wearing a badge.

Beaumont almost laughed out loud. Maywood's marshal looked to be about sixteen, but the Southerner figured he had to be older to have been appointed town marshal. Still, the pint-sized lawman seemed to be a comic figure out of a traveling roadshow, for his ten-gallon hat made his ears lop over, and Beaumont thought it a wonder that the fellow's meatless hips were able to hold up the gun belt that held two big revolvers.

The youthful lawman swaggered up to the column of horses bearing the dead men, stared at them intently, and then informed the Frenchman in a high-pitched voice, "My name's Marshal Ron Castin, and I demand you tell me how and where this happened."

William Louis Beaumont took an immediate dislike to the cocky marshal. What was keeping Vint? "A few miles south of here," he finally answered flatly.

Castin pulled his upper lip over a set of buck teeth in a sneer. Adjusting his oversized Stetson, he coldly reminded the Frenchman, "There was another part to my question, mister. *How* did it happen?"

Beaumont felt the hair bristle on the back of his neck. "These men crept up on my partner and me at dawn this mornin' where we were camped. They were intendin' to kill us and rob us."

Disbelief was evident in the skinny man's eyes. Stepping to the horse that held Bud Mann, he took hold of the cold, stiff dangling right hand of the corpse. Fingering the large diamond ring, he spoke back over his bony shoulder, "Why would a man who could afford a diamond like this one find it necessary to rob someone?"

Irritation crawled on the Frenchman's skin. Had the arrogant young lawman approached him properly, William Louis Beaumont would have answered his questions civilly, explaining about the card game and the cheating gambler. But Castin's haughty attitude made him bristle. "How should I know?" he asked snidely. "Why don't you ask him?"

The marshal's face turned beet red. Whipping out his gun, he pointed it at Beaumont and commanded, "Climb down off that horse!"

"What for?" demanded Beaumont, his temper rising.

"Because I said so, and I am the law in this town!" barked Castin. As if suddenly remembering something, he then demanded, "Where's your partner?"

"That's what I've been wonderin'," mumbled Beaumont, dismounting.

"I didn't hear what you said, mister!" blustered the marshal.

Towering over the little lawman, the Rebel growled, "I said my partner's in the funeral parlor. We're tryin' to get rid of these bodies so we can get back on the road."

"What's your name?" pressed Castin, waving the black muzzle at him.

"William Louis Beaumont," came the reply quickly. "And to save you from the next question, I'm from New Orleans."

A surly look darkened Castin's eyes. "What's your partner's name?"

"Vint Lonegan—and *he's* from Pawtucket, Rhode Island."

Castin held the gun on Beaumont and stepped to Bud Mann's body again, lifting up the hand that bore the diamond ring. "Now, I'm asking once more. Why would a man who could afford a diamond like this be a robber?"

William Louis Beaumont checked his impulse to take the kid's gun away from him and slap his face. Narrowing his black eyes, he snarled, "Has it occurred to you, Marshal, that he might have taken that ring from someone in a robbery?"

Castin's face went blank. "Oh. Well, I suppose he

could have at that"—his face hardened—"but I doubt it. Unbuckle your gun belt."

"Are you charging me with somethin'?" demanded Beaumont.

"Murder," came the cold reply.

"Aw, now look, Marshal," drawled the Southerner in protest, "this is ridiculous. You—"

"Did you and your partner kill these men?"

"Yes, we did. But it wasn't murder. We were only defendin' our lives and our property."

Castin's eyes widened. "Do you think I'm stupid? Looks more like you ambushed 'em to me! How could two men take out six in a head-on gunfight?"

Beaumont replied sardonically, "Sure. We ambushed them, then brought them in here to give them a nice burial."

Just then, Vint Lonegan came through the door of the funeral parlor, followed by a silver-haired man. Lonegan's face stiffened at the sight of the marshal holding a gun on his friend. "What's this, Marshal?" he asked.

Castin pulled his other gun, lining it on Lonegan. "Get those hands in the air, mister!" he snapped. "You and your partner here are under arrest for murder!"

"We're *what*? Beau, didn't you explain to the marshal what happened?"

"I did," sighed the Frenchman, "but he seems to think we ambushed these fellows. Where've you been, anyway?"

"Waiting for Mr. Carruthers to finish whittling a coffin."

The undertaker nodded at Beaumont as he stepped close to Castin and lectured, "Now, Ronnie, you're doing it again . . . overreacting. Don't you think it might be better if—"

"I'm the law in this town, and I'll handle it, Mr. Carruthers!" cut in the cocky little lawman.

The undertaker raised his eyes and shook his head.

"Marshal, we didn't murder these men," Lonegan said bluntly. "And even if we did, your jurisdiction ends at either end of this town. These men were killed out on the prairie."

"The bodies are in my town now, mister!" blared Castin. "You two get your gun belts off! You're going to my jail!"

"Look," said Lonegan, irritation evident in his voice, "I'm Captain Vint Lonegan of the U.S. Army, and let me tell you, you're making a big mistake. You are hindering official government business. I have identification in my saddlebags."

"Hmpf!" snorted Castin. "If you're an Army captain, where's your uniform? Don't bother to answer. I won't believe you, anyway. Anyone can make up false identification papers. Now, you two drop your gun belts, or I'll drill you where you stand!"

Lonegan looked over at Beaumont. The two men read each others' eyes, knowing that the other was also thinking of a way to get out of the predicament without resorting to drastic measures. Suddenly the undertaker suggested, "Perhaps, Captain Lonegan, you should not resist our young marshal's arrest. Relinquish your guns, and I'll talk with him when things have settled down."

Shrugging, the officer complied, as did the Frenchman. Moments later, holding one of his revolvers on them, Ron Castin ushered the two men into his office, his prisoners' gun belts draped over his shoulder. Dropping the gun belts on his desk, he then guided them toward the cell area.

William Louis Beaumont gave Vint Lonegan a dismal look and growled, "You and your dumb degree of dignity."

"I didn't know it was going to lead to a stupid situation like this," Lonegan said defensively.

"Shut up, you two!" rasped Castin. "Go on. Head for the cells."

Beaumont saw by the agitation written all over the

big captain's face that he was going to do something. The Frenchman's body tensed for what was coming.

They passed through the narrow door into a short hallway leading to the cells, Beaumont going first. Without warning, Lonegan did a quick sidestep and seized the wrist of the marshal's gun hand. Jerking him forward with a savage yank, he slammed his head into the bars of the nearest cell. Castin's knees buckled, but he started to resist. Lonegan slammed him into the bars again, harder.

The revolver clattered to the floor, and Ron Castin crumpled in a heap with a bleeding nose. Beaumont stroked his mustache and looked up at his friend with a look of irony on his face.

"Well, something had to be done," Lonegan remarked, grinning sheepishly.

"If you hadn't, I would've," drawled the Southerner.

Quickly, they bound and gagged the little lawman and locked him in a cell. Leaving a note on the desk for Castin to check with Colonel Donald Harrington at Fort McPherson for verification of his identity, Lonegan stepped out into the bright sunlight with his friend.

Undertaker Carruthers was removing the third body from its horse when the two men approached. As they vaulted into their saddles, Carruthers paused, puffing from exertion, and said, "Ronnie change his mind?"

"Yes, sir," answered Beaumont. "The captain convinced him that he'd been a little impetuous."

Carruthers laughed. "It's the story of his life. Kid's barely twenty-one. He's wanted to be a lawman in the worst way ever since I can remember. Tried all over these parts, but nobody'd take him. His uncle is chairman of our town council and owns nearly the whole town—so we got stuck with little Ronnie."

"Well, maybe someday he'll grow up," Lonegan quipped.

Hoisting the body onto his shoulder and turning to carry it inside, the silver-haired undertaker sighed. "I sure hope so."

With a wave, the two men rode out of town.

Chapter Three

Although it was still early in May, the morning sun was quite warm, and the residents of both the town of Lewellen, Nebraska, situated on the north bank of the wide North Platte River, and the Bickford farm, lying in a shallow valley nine miles north of town, sensed the coming summer. Mary Jane Bickford hummed a tune as she scrubbed her wash in a large galvanized tub at the back of the farmhouse. Hearing the angered squawk of a chicken, followed by the laughter of her six-year-old twin sons, she turned and wiped her soapy hands on her apron and then used them to emphasize her words. "I told you boys not to tease that rooster!" she warned, a scowl on her lovely face. "Now, you go find something else to do, or when your father returns from the fields, I'll have to tell him how you've misbehaved!"

Danny and Davey Bickford reluctantly left the ruffled rooster to himself and headed across the yard for the swing that dangled from the limb of a cottonwood tree. As Danny slung his leg over the board seat of the swing, his attention was drawn to movement on a nearby hilltop. Ten bronze-bodied men were silhouetted against the flawless blue sky as they sat their pinto ponies, looking toward the farmhouse.

"Look, Davey!" gasped the towheaded Danny. "Indians!"

Davey Bickford's eyes bulged with fear, and he grabbed his brother's arm to race back to their mother's side. "Mama!" the young boy shouted as they ran. "Indians, Mama! Indians are comin' after us!"

The young mother let the garment she was scrubbing fall into the tub, and she turned and looked at her terrified boys. They reached her side, and she wiped her hands, putting her arms around them protectively and reassuringly and looking in the direction her sons were pointing. Finding the dark figures on the hillside, Mary Jane softly explained, "I told you, the Cheyenne will not hurt white people anymore. Their chief has promised the Army we won't be bothered, so you needn't be afraid."

Jack Bickford's wife would not let on to her frightened youngsters that she still was intimidated by the sight of Indians even though the Hotamitanui Cheyenne chief, Burning Sun, had signed a peace treaty a year and a half previously, and things had been quiet since then—or at least they had been until recently. The last time the Bickfords had gone to town, they had heard that a band of Cheyenne had raided and burned several farms in the area. But Mary Jane reminded herself that that had been over two months ago, and surely if there had been any further trouble, they would have heard of it.

The half-naked riders were making their way down the hill, the feathers in their headbands dancing in the breeze. When they were within a hundred yards of the farmhouse, Mary Jane's innate fear got the better of her, and she told her sons in a voice she hoped sounded more lighthearted than she felt, "Boys, I want you to go into the house. Walk. Don't run."

Davey looked up and studied his mother's face, then declared, "You're *afraid*, Mama. They *are* going to hurt us, aren't they?"

Danny began to whimper.

"No, honey," Mary Jane told him, wishing his father were there. "Everything will be all right."

"Then why can't we stay here with you?" asked Danny, looking up at her with tear-filled eyes.

"It's . . . it's just better that you both be in the house. Go on. Do as I say."

Reluctantly the twins left their mother and entered the house.

Mary Jane's heart was pounding as the Indians drew nearer. Forcing herself to behave casually, although watching them from the corner of her eye, she returned to her washing chore, plunging her hands into the hot, soapy wash water.

The band of white men, their bodies painted a copper color and each carrying Cheyenne arrows in a quiver and bows in their hands, watched the domestic scene below. "That's the Bickford place down there," Todd Dressler announced, adjusting his Cheyenne headband.

"Just burn it, that's all, right, Corporal?" queried one of the men.

"Rufus!" snapped Dressler, shifting slightly on the back of his borrowed pinto pony. "How many times do I have to tell you not to call me corporal?"

"Sorry. I keep forgettin'."

"Well, don't forget!" growled the ex-corporal. "I left the stinking Army because I hate everything about it. And as I recall, so do you."

The former trooper nodded, brushing at his sweating brow.

"Be careful!" warned Dressler. "You'll wipe that paint off!" He glared at him for a moment and then said, "Now, as to your question, that's right. We just set the place on fire. No killing—unless that farmer decides to be stupid and give us trouble. If he does, and we have to kill him, be sure to leave his wife alive so's she can tell the Army it was Cheyennes who burned them out."

Dressler then faced forward, muttering, "I don't know how them Indians can stand to ride all the time without a saddle." Giving his men a nod, he ordered, "Let's go."

The masquerading riders trotted into the yard and reined to a halt. Mary Jane Bickford straightened and turned as the "Indians" massed around her, and she looked up at them wordlessly, her uneasiness apparent.

Lowering his voice and speaking in pidgin English, hoping to sound convincing, Todd Dressler asked, "Where is husband?"

Mary Jane swallowed hard and replied, "He's . . . uh . . . he's close by. He's . . . uh . . . he's working over near the barn."

The ex-corporal twisted around and stared at the barn for a long moment.

The woman licked her lips nervously. "He's th-there somewhere," she assured him, her voice breaking in obvious fear.

Dressler's head whipped around, and he barked, "You lie!"

The woman's hands started shaking, and she choked, "What do you want?"

Ignoring her question, Dressler spoke to the painted man just behind him and grunted, "Set house on fire."

Mary Jane Bickford's hand went to her mouth and she screeched, "You can't do that! Your chief signed a treaty and you're supposed to leave us alone! Please!"

Todd Dressler eyed her stonily as one of the ex-troopers swung a deerskin-breeches-clad leg over his pinto's back and slid to the ground. Matches in hand, he started past Mary Jane toward the house. From the kitchen came the fearful cry of one of the boys, and the young mother's instinct to protect her young immediately surfaced. Grabbing a small pan on the ground beside the washtub, she dipped it into the hot, soapy water and hurled it at the man's face. The lye in the soap burned his eyes and, howling, he dropped the matches and threw his hands to his eyes.

Mary Jane Bickford suddenly gasped, for the strong soap washed off some of the paint, exposing the man's white skin. Drawing a ragged breath, she whispered, "You're not Indians!" She turned and ran toward the house, screaming, "Run, boys! Run!"

Cursing loudly, Todd Dressler slipped off his pony and reached for an arrow from the quiver on his back and started stringing it into his bow. He coldly declared, "We can't let her live now, or the whole scheme is over."

The young woman reached the back porch, gesticulating wildly at her twin sons who stood staring out the kitchen window, their eyes huge with terror. "Hurry! Out the front! Run!" she shrieked.

The bowstring hummed, and the arrow struck Mary Jane between the shoulder blades as she grabbed the doorknob. She stiffened, then staggered and fell backward. The weight of her body shoved the arrow completely through her chest. Screams from the boys could be heard through the closed window.

"What about the kids?" one of Dressler's men asked.

"They saw it all," Dressler replied. "A couple of you go in there and take care of 'em."

Minutes later the ex-Army corporal and his band of cutthroats mounted up and looked back at their handiwork. The house and barn were ablaze, pillars of black smoke billowing toward the sky, and the body of Mary Jane Bickford had been dragged far enough away from the blazing structure to make sure it did not catch fire. The Cheyenne arrow in her body would be sufficient evidence to ignite the ire of the U.S. Army against Chief Burning Sun's people.

Turning to leave, the men saw a wagon racing

across a field from the south, bouncing and bounding toward the homestead.

"Todd!" shouted one of the men. "It's the farmer!"

Jack Bickford was snapping the reins at the team, driving them full speed. Drawing near, he held the reins with one hand while reaching to the floor of the wagon for his rifle.

"Kill him!" Dressler shouted to his men. "Everybody notch your arrows! Let him have it!"

Bickford suddenly yanked back on the reins, drawing the wagon to a jerky stop. But he was within range of the "Indians," and eight arrows sliced through the air, six of them hitting him. Buckling as the arrows thunked into his body, he dropped the rifle without getting off a shot and peeled headfirst to the ground.

Todd Dressler nudged his horse forward until he was beside the dead farmer. Laughing, he exclaimed, "He looks like a porcupine, boys! Just wait'll the Army gets a gander at this! They'll be ready to launch a full-scale war against Burning Sun!"

When the ex-corporal and the other deserters thundered into the corral of their hideout some twelve miles southeast of Lewellen, Todd Dressler noted the four horses tied to a hitching rail near the back porch of the old deserted farmhouse. This meant Clete Holman and his henchmen were inside the house.

Dressler and his men led their pintos inside the old barn to ensure that no one would see them. The abandoned farmstead had served them well as a base for carrying out their nefarious scheme, for the place was a couple of miles off the beaten track and was nestled in a thicket of drooping willows and towering cottonwoods, providing additional cover for them as they embarked upon and returned from their clandestine activities.

As the group left the barn and walked through the corral, four rough-looking men filed through the back door of the house and stood on the dilapidated porch waiting for them. Smiling at the tall, muscular leader as he drew near, Dressler commented, "I guess you fellas didn't have any trouble finding the place."

"Your map was perfect," responded Clete Holman. "We were gettin' a little worried about you, though."

"Just out doing our job," Dressler assured him. "We ran into a little trouble that slowed us down." He explained what had happened, concluding, "The Cheyenne will get the blame, all right."

"Good," Holman grunted, nodding. Gesturing at Dressler's men, who were standing by the water trough washing the paint off their bodies, he asked, "My idea's workin', ain't it?"

"Like a charm," replied Dressler, pulling off his headband. "I think old Burning Sun's mighty fed up with the Army's saying he's breaking the treaty. He'll be ready to fight when he gets his hands on those six hundred rifles you're bringing in—or at least that's what the Indians supplying us with all this Cheyenne equipment are telling me."

Holman laughed. "Really lights a fuse under the old boy for his warriors to be accused of attackin' wagon trains and stagecoaches and burnin' farms, don't it?"

Dressler nodded. "Especially when he's tried so hard to keep that treaty. Burning Sun's rode herd on his people, trying to keep things peaceful with the whites. He really meant to stand by that treaty. Uh . . . that is, meant to up until lately."

Clete Holman laughed appreciatively at Dressler's joke. "You and your boys have strained that treaty to the snapping point, just like Three Hands thought. He told me the old chief really lost his temper a few days ago when the colonel from Fort McPherson rode into his village and insisted it was Cheyennes pulling all these raids." Grinning, he added, "Almost jammed his peace pipe down the colonel's throat!"

Dressler chuckled with glee.

Holman scratched his stubbly beard, asking the ex-corporal, "Have you met Three Hands yet?"

"Nope. It was a few of his warriors who brought the ponies and Indian gear for us to use on these raids. But I remember hearing Colonel Harrington say that this Three Hands is really savage."

"No exaggeration," Holman responded, grinning. "Which makes him perfect for our deal. He's Burning Sun's favorite warrior, and men who've seen him in hand-to-hand combat say he's so strong and so fast, he seems to have an extra hand. I understand that's where he got his name—Three Hands."

"He's also Burning Sun's main subchief, according to the colonel," commented Dressler. "There's no doubt when Burning Sun dies, Three Hands'll become chief of the Dog Men."

"Dog Men?"

"Yeah. The Hotamitanui band."

"Funny, I never asked Three Hands about any of that Indian stuff." He grinned broadly, adding, "All I was interested in was cuttin' a deal. So, is that a separate Cheyenne tribe?"

"No. The Cheyenne aren't like most of the other Indians. The Cheyenne nation isn't made up of different tribes. It's made up of ten 'bands,' and each band has its own chief, with a main subchief who's gotta prove himself fierce and brave in the face of battle."

Dressler paused to let that information sink in and then continued, "The Dog Men band is like the military. It produces the greatest warriors and the best fighters in the Cheyenne nation. They aren't called Dog Men for nothin', 'cause when they do battle, they go at it like wild dogs. They're plenty tough—and Three Hands is the toughest of 'em all."

Holman lit a cigarette and took a deep pull, and then asked, "Is there a main chief over the whole nation of Cheyenne, or is it made up of ten chiefs?"

"Ten chiefs."

"So the treaty that Burning Sun signed with the colonel at Fort McPherson really only holds the Hota—How do you say it?"

"Hotamitanui."

Holman shook his head and muttered, "It's a lot easier to say 'Dog Men.' Anyway, only the Dog Men bunch are under the treaty then?"

"Well, yes and no. Usually whenever one of the chiefs makes peace with the Army in an area, the others honor it." He sneered and then remarked, "And the opposite also holds true."

Grinning, Holman said, "So old Burning Sun's really upset at the Army, huh? I guess he'll be plenty happy to have the kind of weapons I'm bringin' in."

"Gonna make us a whole lot richer, too," put in Dick Swope, who stood on the porch next to his boss. Spitting a brown stream of tobacco juice into the ground, he added, "In real gold, at that."

Todd Dressler's eyebrows arched. Looking at Holman he said, "The Cheyenne are paying for those six hundred rifles and all that ammunition with gold?"

"Sure are," confirmed Clete Holman with greed in his eyes. "Shiny gold nuggets. Three Hands assured me that's how he'd be payin'."

"Where'd they get it?" Dressler queried.

"Nobody knows," replied Holman, flicking ashes from his cigarette. "Leastwise, I guess, nobody outside Burning Sun's clan. But who cares where they're gettin' it as long as we get our share, eh?"

Shrugging his shoulders and smiling broadly, the ex-corporal said, "I don't. Sure am glad I ran into you again after all these years, Clete. My boys and I'll make more money on this job than we'd have made in ten years in the Army." Wiping paint from his face, he commented, "Guess I'd better get this stuff washed off before Three Hands gets here."

* * *

At sunset, a large group of Cheyenne warriors rode into the farmyard, with Three Hands at the head. Todd Dressler and his men immediately stood with their mouths agape, clearly in awe of the muscular brave, whose body was like that of a statue. There was also an evilness about the man, and it was evident to anyone looking at him that he was cold, calculating, and as mean as a teased rattler. Far from resenting the impression everyone had of him, Three Hands was pleased; it made it easier to intimidate those who were weak and to sway those who were unsure.

Clete Holman stepped off the porch as Three Hands slid from his horse. "Welcome, my friend," Holman declared expansively. "We appreciate the horses and equipment you sent us. I want you to meet the man who's been leadin' the raids." Smiling, he added, "When he's painted up, he makes a good Cheyenne." Motioning to Dressler, he ordered, "Come over here, Todd."

Walking toward the subchief, the ex-corporal eyed him closely. Three Hands stood stiffly with his strong arms folded across his chest, but his dark and mysterious eyes focused on Dressler's face, boring into the former soldier.

Introducing the two, Holman said, "Three Hands, this is Todd Dressler. He's an old friend of mine. We grew up in the same town."

The subchief did not offer his hand. He acknowledged Dressler with a slight nod then said in a deep, resonant voice, "Todd Dressler and his men have done well. United States Army has angered my chief, and Burning Sun believes bluecoats accuse Cheyenne of raids only to bring war. My chief will soon be angry enough to put on war paint—then white eyes will die! White eyes want Cheyenne land? We will give it to him. We will *bury* him in it!"

Clete Holman chuckled hollowly. Elbowing

Dressler, he said, "Of course, he don't mean us, Todd. He means them soldiers."

Dressler smiled weakly, and it was evident from the expression on his face that he found the Indian frightening. Three Hands had an air about him of a relentless predator—but unlike any other animal, this human one was cold-blooded and blackhearted.

What neither white man knew was that Three Hands was masterminding the overthrow of Burning Sun and the takeover of the Hotamitanui band, and he was using any means at his disposal to do so. He had lied to Clete Holman in telling him that Burning Sun would soon be angry enough to put on war paint, for not only was the Hotamitanui chief *not* ready to declare war on the whites, Three Hands doubted that the chief ever would. But while most of his people would deem Three Hands's actions as traitorous, the subchief saw them as the proper response to an aging chief gone soft.

Three Hands felt great resentment toward Burning Sun for signing a treaty with the hated white men in the first place, believing whites should be dealt with using bullets and arrows, not pieces of paper. If something was not done about it, they would continue to steal Cheyenne land and freedom until both were gone. The muscular young subchief vowed to stop the tide, and the best way to do so was to eliminate Burning Sun and give the Dog Men warriors a new leader—one who would inspire them to rid their sacred land of the palefaced intruders and one who did not fear the greedy white men. Three Hands would be that man.

The Hotamitanui people were becoming increasingly antagonized by the Army's insistence of laying responsibility for the recent raids at their feet. Though Burning Sun was trying hard to keep them cool, anger and resentment were slowly rising to a fever pitch. Already Three Hands had enlisted forty likeminded Dog Men to follow him. When he eliminated Burning Sun, he would have them all, and soon the other bands of Cheyenne would follow Three Hands's example. In a short time, the entire Cheyenne nation would be roused into a full-scale uprising against the whites.

Three Hands was working on a way to kill Burning Sun and lay the blame on the whites. He would time it so that he had Clete Holman's six hundred repeating rifles in hand when the chief was eliminated. Believing their beloved old chief to have been murdered by white men, the Dog Men would be more than ready to go on the warpath—especially when their new chief presented them with modern repeating rifles.

Three Hands laughed to himself. Let Clete Holman think the subchief was acting for Chief Burning Sun in the purchase of the rifles and ammunition. The end result would be the same: The well-armed Dog Men would wipe out Fort McPherson first, causing the other bands to rally. Soon the entire Cheyenne nation would eliminate every Army post on their ancestral land.

Clete Holman broke into the warrior's reverie. Holding up a shiny, nickle-plated Spencer .44 caliber seven-shot repeater rifle, Holman grinned and declared, "Three Hands, this is a special gift for you. A token of goodwill."

The Indian's eyes widened as he beheld the magnificent weapon, and a slight smile tugged at one end of his stern mouth.

Still grinning, Holman explained, "The six hundred I'm bringing in don't have the nickel plate, but otherwise they're exactly the same."

The muscular Indian examined the Spencer with admiration, turning it over and over in his hands.

"It's gettin' dark out here," Holman announced. "Let's go inside and talk details. Todd, you come in with us."

Three Hands turned to his warriors and told them to dismount. He explained he would briefly discuss further business with the gunrunner, and then they would be on their way. So saying, he turned back and followed the two white men into the old farmhouse.

Floorboards creaked under their weight, and the rooms were musty and dank. Clete Holman flared a match and touched it to the wick of an oil lamp, and the musty odor was momentarily covered by the sulfur smell from the burning match. Holman raised the wick, and yellow light spilled across the room, throwing elusive shadows against the walls.

The gunrunner motioned to a chair and said, "Have a seat, Three Hands."

The Indian waited till Holman had sat down before doing so himself, leaning the shiny new Spencer against his leg. Holman then told the subchief, "The rifles and ammunition are comin' into Nebraska on a wagon train. The wagonmaster is a close friend of mine."

Three Hands grunted, "It is said that Army is inspecting wagon trains. They know of other repeater rifles being brought here."

"I'm aware of that," countered Holman, leaning back in the chair. "But all the inspectin's been done after the wagon trains have passed the town of North Platte 'cause the Army's too shorthanded to get to them before that. I've made arrangements with the Wells Fargo agent in North Platte to meet my friend's wagon train east of town under cover of darkness. There are twelve wooden crates holding fifty rifles each, plus other boxes containing three thousand rounds of ammunition, all marked TOOLS. They'll be stashed in the Wells Fargo barn in town. Then they'll be loaded onto the next three stages running between North Platte and Scottsbluff. I'll pick 'em up at the town of Oshkosh."

Holman looked at the warrior, who nodded both his approval and his understanding. Continuing, the gunrunner said, "Working under cover of darkness, me and my men'll put the guns and ammunition on rafts and float 'em on the North Platte River to a small island about ten miles straight north of here. The island's got heavy brush and tree cover, and it's right out in the middle of the river, which is about a hundred and fifty feet wide there. It's the perfect place to stash the shipment. When we've got all the guns and ammunition on the island, you can bring the gold and we'll make the swap right there."

"How long will this take?" queried the Indian.

"Once the guns have been taken off the wagon train, we're lookin' at six days," answered Holman. "The stagecoaches run every other day."

The Indian eyed Holman with admiration. "My friend Clete Holman is plenty smart."

The gunrunner smiled and said, "In my business you have to be."

"How soon is wagon train expected?"

"Any day now."

"How will Three Hands know when rifles are ready to be picked up at island?"

"In a week, send one of your braves here to the hideout. As soon as the crates have been stashed, one of Dressler's men will return here and tell your man. He can ride like the wind back to you, and as soon as you can come with the gold, the guns are yours."

Three Hands smiled and stood up. "Chief Burning Sun will be pleased to learn that everything is going as planned," he lied easily. The gunrunner stood up as well, and the two men shook hands Indian-style. Narrowing his black eyes, the warrior mused, "Three Hands wonders . . ."

"About what?"

"Does it not bother you that selling rifles to Dog Men will mean many of your white brothers will die?"

The avaricious gunrunner laughed heartily and shrugged. "Everybody has to die sooner or later. Business is business—and gold is gold!"

Moments later, Three Hands and his warriors mounted up and rode away in the darkness. Out on the plains, the warrior laughed to himself, thinking, *Like all white men, Clete Holman is a fool. But he is right about one thing: Everyone must die sooner or later. For him and his foolish followers it will be sooner . . . at the hands of Dog Men!*

Chapter Four

It was growing dark when Captain Vint Lonegan and William Louis Beaumont saw the outline of Fort McPherson's stockade on the horizon. It had taken longer to reach the fort than Lonegan had hoped, and the pair was extremely impatient to finally reach their destination.

William Louis Beaumont turned to the man riding beside him and suggested, "I'm real tired of this saddle, so what do you say we get this over with and put these horses to a gallop?"

"Okay," agreed Lonegan, "but we'll walk them the last quarter mile or so. If we come charging in, some sentry might think we're Indians and start shooting— and, I must say, I'm in no mood to get shot at tonight."

Beaumont chuckled. "You remind me of old Grandmother Beaumont."

"Your *grandmother*?" the captain declared.

"Yep. Always did things real careful and cautious, same as you. Stood her well, though. She lived to be a hundred and three."

Laughing, Lonegan retorted, "Well, I've been called a lot of things in the course of my life, but never has anyone accused me of being like his grandmother!" He laughed again, then said, "Okay, Rebel, let's ride!"

Without waiting for acknowledgment, he kicked his mount's side.

The silhouette of Fort McPherson drew up fast as the horses thundered across the dark prairie, and when Lonegan determined they were about a quarter mile from the fort, they reined the animals to a walk. Presently they could make out the sentries standing on the catwalk above the gate, and before the soldiers challenged them, Lonegan shouted, "Ho, the fort! Captain Vint Lonegan coming in!"

"Approach the gate," came the reply.

A lantern flared quickly and the two men rode into a soft ring of yellow light. One of the three sentries who studied the two men on horseback finally called, "Well, it's you, sure enough, Captain Lonegan! Welcome back. Glad to see you. Who's your companion?"

"William Louis Beaumont. He's a friend of mine," replied Lonegan. "He's traveling with me for personal reasons."

"If he's a friend of yours," responded the sentry, motioning for a man on the ground to open the gate, "he's got to be okay, sir. Incidentally, is the colonel expecting you?"

"Yes. I sent him a wire several days ago."

The two men rode through the gate and dismounted, and a sergeant led them across the hard-packed parade ground to the commandant's quarters. As they approached Colonel Donald Harrington's residence, Lonegan smiled at how swiftly information was passed along. Standing outside, illuminated by a lamp hanging on a porch post and obviously already alerted to Lonegan's arrival, Harrington was waiting for the captain.

A tall, slender man of fifty, the colonel was a stately figure. The lamplight glinted off the highly polished brass buttons of his uniform as well as the streaks of silver in his thick, dark hair. "Good evening, gentlemen," Harrington declared with a smile. He dismissed the sergeant, then extended his hand to Lonegan and said, "Good to see you again, Vint."

"Thank you, sir," Lonegan responded, grinning. Turning slightly, he laid a hand on the Frenchman's shoulder. "Colonel, I would like you to meet my friend, William Louis Beaumont from New Orleans."

Beaumont met the colonel's grasp. "Happy to make your acquaintance, sir," he drawled, flashing a smile. "The captain has told me much about you."

"All good, I hope," quipped Harrington.

"Most if it, sir," Beaumont replied with a twinkle in his eye.

Harrington laughed, then cocked his head and boldly assessed the Southerner. He finally asked, "From the way you're standing at attention, Beaumont, would I be correct in assuming you were in the Confederate Army?"

"You are correct, sir. I was a Rebel lieutenant—but don't worry. I don't hate Yankees anymore. I just feel sorry for them."

Harrington arched his eyebrows. "Why's that?"

A sly grin formed on Beaumont's mouth. "Well, sir, there's just not enough room for everybody to live below the Mason-Dixon line, meanin' some folk are simply forced to live in the north. I feel mighty bad for those of you who can't be Southerners."

The colonel sighed. "Mr. Beaumont, I wish more of your fellow confederates felt as you do. Here it is eighteen sixty-eight, and three years have passed since the war ended—officially, that is. Unfortunately, it has yet to end in the minds and hearts of an awful lot of people." The three men were silent for a long moment, and then Harrington turned to Lonegan and said, "I received your wire, Vint. I have a message for you from Washington."

"Yes, sir. General Payne knew I was on my way here."

"Well," the colonel suggested, "we can handle government business later. I imagine you two are hungry."

"Actually, Colonel, 'starving' would be more accurate," confessed Lonegan. "Would we be able to get something to eat over at the mess hall?"

"You might, but you won't," Harrington replied. "My family and I were about to sit down to the table. We would be honored if you would take your repast with us."

"Oh, we wouldn't want to intrude, sir," insisted Lonegan.

"Nonsense! I'll have it no other way. We'll let you wash and freshen up a bit, and you'll dine with us in exactly one hour."

The weary travelers were shown to their quarters by a young corporal, where they washed off some of the prairie dust and combed their hair. Precisely one hour after leaving Harrington, they knocked on the colonel's door. The commandant invited them in and ushered them to the dining room, which was filled with the aroma of food coming from the kitchen.

Moments later, three women—all brunettes—filed through a door at the opposite end of the room. The first woman was Lila Harrington who, though in her late forties, had retained a youthful look. Behind the lovely Lila were her two stunning daughters—first the oldest, twenty-one-year-old Darlene, and then Marie, who was a mature nineteen. It was evident from the gowns the women wore and from their formal hairdos—an elegant twist in Lila's case and cascading ringlets on Darlene and Marie—that the Harrington woman had dressed with special care in honor of their guests.

The three women greeted Captain Vint Lonegan with warm smiles, each telling him it was good to see him again.

"And I'm delighted to see the three of you," he responded. "You certainly are a sight for sore eyes—and

I think you've all gotten even lovelier since last I saw you."

William Louis Beaumont then turned on his Southern charm. "I presume, Colonel, that these beautiful ladies are your three daughters. As beautiful as *they* are, I can't wait to meet your wife!"

Lila laughed. "Well, whoever you are, young man," she exclaimed merrily, "I like you already!"

"William Louis Beaumont," said the colonel, gesturing at the suave Frenchman, "may I present my wife, Lila, and my daughters, Darlene and Marie."

A typical New Orleans gentleman, Beaumont clicked his heels, bowed before each lady, and pressed their fingers to his lips. "I declare, Colonel, I'd bet you have quite a problem keepin' the young soldiers of Fort McPherson away from your door."

Marie giggled with pleasure while Darlene blushed. The Harrington sisters bore a remarkable resemblance to each other and were a perfect blending of both parents. Darlene's personality was a bit more subdued than that of her sister, but both young ladies were captivating.

During the course of the meal, the strikingly handsome Frenchman dazzled the Harrington women with his wit and charm. Vint Lonegan found Beaumont's performance amusing, and he let his new-found friend dominate the conversation. Still, Lonegan was able to squeeze in a brief explanation of how the two of them had met and why they were traveling together.

When the meal was finished, Lila stood up and said, "I believe you gentlemen have some business to discuss, so if you'll retire to the den, we ladies will attend to these dishes."

The three men rose, and Beaumont turned to the women, telling them effusively, "Ladies, it has been the delight of this humble southern gentleman to dine in the presence of such exquisite beauty. Perhaps in the not-too-distant future, such good fortune shall once again be afforded to this totally overwhelmed and undeserving gentleman."

Lila Harrington laughed. "Mr. Beaumont, you are a sterling example of southern chivalry—and it's a good thing that my husband and his fellow officers were heading up the Union Army and not their wives. Otherwise *we* might have surrendered to such heady charm!"

Chuckling appreciatively, the three men took their leave and went down the hallway to the den.

Colonel Donald Harrington lit his pipe and then gestured to his guests to be seated in a pair of overstuffed chairs. The colonel then pulled a third chair over, facing the others, and sat himself.

Lonegan immediately got to the point, asking Harrington, "Colonel, what was my message from General Payne?"

Removing the pipe from his mouth, the colonel replied, "The wire contained additional orders for you. But before we get to the details of your added assignment, let me say that you're definitely closing in on Clete Holman, whom I understand you've been tracking. I've been kept fully informed about Holman's activities, but I wasn't aware until the wire came that you had been the one assigned to track him. Word is that he passed near here only a few days ago, swinging in from the south and now heading west."

William Louis Beaumont was visibly jolted by the sound of Clete Holman's name. Both the other men saw his reaction, and Harrington asked, "Do you know this man Holman?"

Beaumont sat forward on the edge of the chair. His eyes wide, he responded by querying Lonegan, "The gunrunner you're chasing is Clete Holman?"

"The same," confirmed Lonegan with a nod. "You know him?"

"He's the man *I'm* after!"

It was Lonegan's turn to show surprise. Looking

intently at his companion, he asked, "You owe money to Clete Holman?"

The Frenchman stood up, clearly agitated. "When I said I owed him," he replied bitterly, "I didn't mean money—I meant a debt of vengeance." He paused and then added in a steely voice, "And I always pay my debts."

Harrington and Lonegan glanced at each other, and the captain read the same discomfort in the commandant's eyes that he himself felt. Vint Lonegan then looked up at his traveling companion and asked, "Where did you meet Holman, and what has he done to you?"

The Frenchman stared vacantly into space. "I haven't met him . . . yet. But a good friend of mine was the victim of his brutality. You see, six months ago, Holman and his cronies were in Santa Fe, New Mexico. My friend, Art Sands, got into a dispute with Holman over a woman—actually, it was Art's fiancée—whereupon Art whipped Holman in a fistfight. Later, Holman and his pals abducted Art and took him to an old deserted barn. There they smashed his hands, legs, and feet with a sledgehammer." He paused, breathing hard with fury, and then added, "They mutilated him, cripplin' him for life. He's been left with mangled, useless hands and feet." Beaumont stared down at Lonegan. "I'm goin' to kill him, Vint! If it's the last thing I ever do, I'm goin' to get Holman and his pals!"

Lonegan was silent for a moment and then declared, "I've learned a lot of things about Clete Holman of late—learned that he's a ruthless, greedy outlaw who'll do anything to line his pockets with money, including murdering someone with no more regard than swatting a fly. His selling repeater rifles to the Indians just adds one more evil to his list of wicked deeds. I wouldn't put it past Holman or the men he rides with to cut their own mothers' throats for a dollar, so your friend's story doesn't surprise me. It disgusts me, but it doesn't surprise me."

Colonel Donald Harrington got out of his chair, concern showing in his eyes. "Mr. Beaumont," the commandant began, "you must understand, Holman and his men are federal fugitives. You must not get in the way of our bringing them in."

The Frenchman clearly did not attempt to suppress his fury. "I mean no disrespect, Colonel," he railed, "but I owe Clete Holman for Art Sands, and the entire United States Army could not stop me from findin' Holman and payin' that debt! Don't worry, I'm no murderer. But I guarantee you, I'll kill him—and his pals as well."

Hastily, Harrington stated, "With all due regard to your feelings, Mr. Beaumont—and if Sands were my friend, I'd no doubt feel as you do—I must say again that Holman and his men are federal fugitives. It is Captain Lonegan's job as a federal officer to track them down, arrest them, and bring them in for trial."

Beaumont looked Harrington in the eye and asked, "What if they resist arrest?"

"Then the captain will have to kill them and bring in their corpses," the colonel replied flatly.

"So it doesn't make any difference if they come in warm or cold, just so they're brought in. Right?"

Growing irritated, the colonel replied tartly, "Wrong, Mr. Beaumont. We need them alive if at all possible in order to learn their source of supply and just how they smuggle those guns and ammunition to the hostiles. We have to get to Holman's supplier in order to completely put this trafficking to a halt."

"The colonel's right, Beau," spoke up Lonegan. "Killing Holman and his men won't stop the repeater rifles from being sold to the Indians. There'll be someone else waiting to take up where they left off. We've got to know the source of supply and eliminate it. Strike the snake where it will kill him . . . in the head. If we can take Holman alive, we can sweat the information out of him."

The colonel nodded emphatically. "The reason Holman was in New Mexico was because he's supplying repeater rifles to the Apache. You probably know that in the last three or four months there, a lot of U.S. Cavalry blood has been shed. With those repeaters, the hostiles are almost impossible to stop."

Beaumont regarded the two men silently.

"Holman has come north to do business with the Cheyenne, the Kiowa, and the Sioux," continued the colonel. "There's going to be a virtual bloodbath on these plains if the Indians get their hands on those repeaters. Holman and his supplier must be stopped. I know you want vengeance for your friend, and I can't blame you. But many, many lives are at stake here."

"I understand, Colonel," Beaumont sighed, "but how about letting *me* catch Holman? I guarantee you I can do it. Let me beat the information out of him. Once you have that, he'll be all mine."

Vint Lonegan stood up and looked at Colonel Harrington. The senior officer was openly uneasy about Beaumont's enthusiasm for killing Clete Holman and his cohorts, and Lonegan felt the same way. To the Frenchman he said, "Beau, I know you saved my skin back in McCook, and I owe you a lot, but I am oath-bound to my job and duty-bound to my superiors to bring them in alive, if possible."

Shaking his head, Beaumont stated, "And I am oath-bound to Art Sands to see Clete Holman pay for what he did."

The captain was quiet for a few moments, mulling over an idea. Finally he turned to Harrington and said, "Colonel, I have a suggestion."

"I'm listening," Fort McPherson's commandant responded.

"Beau was a lieutenant in the Confederate Army. What if you were to wire U.S. Army headquarters in

Washington and obtain authority to give him a special commission to assist me in the pursuit and apprehension of Clete Holman and his men? As a federal officer, Beau would be obligated to bring in Holman and his men alive if possible."

"Hey, now wait a minute!" protested the Southerner. "I don't mind travelin' with you to hunt down Holman, but this commission stuff—I just don't know."

"You don't have much choice!" snapped Captain Vint Lonegan with a glint in his eye. "If you insist on continuing your search for Holman—who is a federal fugitive—as a civilian, I can have you arrested for obstruction of justice. You will be incarcerated in Fort McPherson's guardhouse until Holman is apprehended."

The Rebel's eyes narrowed. "You wouldn't."

The Yankee lowered his head until his nose was less than three inches away from Beaumont's. "Try me," he growled.

"Then I'll take the commission."

Lonegan grinned victoriously. "I knew you were smart."

"Very well," agreed the colonel expansively, clapping each of the younger men on a shoulder, "I'll wire Washington first thing in the morning. We should have it done before the noon hour."

Regarding Lonegan wryly, Beaumont muttered, "You remind me of a cousin of mine."

"Oh?"

"Yeah. He was just as crafty as you are."

Lonegan laughed. "First I remind you of your grandmother, now I remind you of your cousin. Well, at least you're keeping it in the family. But it doesn't say much for your relatives, does it?"

The three men had a good laugh. When the laughter subsided, Lonegan remarked, "Colonel, you said General Payne had given me an added assignment."

"Yes. Several weeks ago, Corporal Todd Dressler

and nine other troopers deserted their squad while out on patrol, killing their lieutenant and sergeant in the process."

Shaking his head in disgust, Lonegan put in, "I take it someone lived long enough to tell the story when they were found."

"Precisely. Sergeant Finch had four slugs in him, but somehow he managed to survive just long enough to return to the fort and describe what happened."

"I assume we have descriptions of these yellow-bellied cowards," commented Lonegan angrily.

"I can provide you with them, yes," assured the colonel.

"Do you have any idea which way they headed?"

"Finch didn't tell us," responded Harrington. "But there's more, Captain. A series of hit-and-run attacks have taken place on farms, ranches, stagecoaches, and wagon trains, which began shortly after Dressler and his men deserted. In each case, the raiders consisted of a band of Cheyenne."

Lonegan was stunned. "Are you telling me that Chief Burning Sun has gone back on his peace treaty?"

"I had that same question, Vint," said the colonel, "so I decided to ask him personally if he had broken the treaty."

"Wasn't it you, sir, who negotiated the treaty with the Dog Men?"

"That's correct. A year and a half ago—in fact, not long after you were last here. I got to know the old chief well, and I believed him to be a man of his word."

Lonegan was silent for a long moment, staring off into the distance. Then, rousing himself, he asked, "So what was your conclusion?"

Harrington began to pace. "Nearly three weeks ago I assembled a squad and rode to Burning Sun's village. When I confronted the chief with the accusations—eyewitness accounts from survivors—the chief insisted he had not ordered the raids and, further, knew absolutely nothing about them. Things got a little sticky. Some of his braves were angry that I would even insinuate the treaty had been broken, saying I was insulting the chief. You've heard of Three Hands, the chief's top warrior?"

Vint Lonegan's mouth pulled into a grim line. "Yeah, I know Three Hands," he replied fiercely and bitterly.

The other two men stared at the captain, clearly taken aback by his response, but when Lonegan did not elaborate, they said nothing.

Harrington then continued, "Well, he declared that he doubted there were any raids at all. Accused me of making them up just so I could start trouble with the Cheyenne nation."

"That's an absurd idea," Lonegan muttered, shaking his head.

"Of course it is. Anyway, Burning Sun vehemently denied the charges, and I made it quite clear that I believed him. Then I suggested there might be some rebels amongst the Dog Men who were doing it without his knowledge . . . or that it might be some warriors from one of the other Cheyenne bands."

"What'd he say to that?" Beaumont spoke up, clearly intrigued by the narrative.

"He scowled at me for a moment, then assured me he would make a thorough investigation. Four days ago, he rode in here and told me that he had checked matters out, and he was certain that no Cheyenne were doing the raiding."

"If the old boy is telling the truth," put in Lonegan, "there's a skunk in the woodpile somewhere."

"I'm convinced of that," agreed Harrington, "because I believe Burning Sun is telling the truth. Even Three Hands told me he believed somebody was pulling the wool over everybody's eyes."

"You mean Three Hands finally agreed that the raids were actually taking place?" asked Lonegan.

"Yes. But he also assured me that the Cheyenne want peace with us."

"Well, if it's not Cheyenne doing the raiding," said Lonegan, "it's somebody impersonating Cheyenne." He peered at the colonel intently and then declared, "Dressler and his men!"

The colonel nodded. "Exactly my conclusion. The troubles began shortly after they deserted, and every report by survivors included the fact that there are ten men in the raiding party."

Lonegan angrily punched his fist into his palm. "Those dirty vermin are painting themselves up to appear as Cheyenne. But why?"

"That's the puzzler," responded Harrington. "For the life of me, I can't figure it out."

William Louis Beaumont stroked his mustache thoughtfully and then asked, "Colonel, do you suppose they figure it's a good cover-up for robbery? Instead of wearin' masks, they masquerade as Indians?"

"That can't be it," countered Harrington, shaking his head slowly. "Nothing is ever taken; in fact, they destroy property. They usually set buildings on fire or torch stagecoaches and prairie schooners. But they steal nothing. And if anyone interferes, they're wounded or killed."

"Do they always leave some survivors?"

Harrington nodded. "Almost always. Only in two cases did they kill everybody. But even then, they left plenty of arrows behind to show clearly that Cheyenne had done it."

"Then they're definitely wanting us to believe the Cheyenne are doing it," Vint Lonegan mused.

"It would certainly appear so," confirmed the colonel. "But the big question is still staring us in the face: why?"

The big captain thought a moment and then said, "Even if what we're assuming is correct, Colonel, we've still got us a mangy skunk in the woodpile. Am I correct in assuming that these raiders are outfitted to the hilt? I mean, besides having Cheyenne arrows, they have pinto ponies and Cheyenne clothing?"

"Bows, arrows, spears, headbands, feathers, leggings, moccasins, and pintos," Harrington affirmed.

"Could it be another tribe just tryin' to get the Cheyenne in hot water?" suggested Beaumont. "I mean like the Crow. I understand the Crow and the Cheyenne are bitter enemies."

"It's a possibility," conceded Harrington. "But with always the same number of men in the raiding party, it's highly improbable. I have a real gut feeling that it's Dressler."

"Then our skunk is in the Cheyenne woodpile," Lonegan breathed. "Somebody is supplying Dressler and his bunch with Cheyenne articles."

"That's what it would add up to," the Colonel sighed, shrugging. He took a long pull on his pipe and then began pacing back and forth again. "But the thing beats the devil out of me. Why would a Cheyenne want to make his people look bad, not to mention risk shedding the blood of his own kin?"

Captain Vint Lonegan slowly shook his head and then responded, "Well, sir, I guess all our questions will be answered when we bring Dressler and his pals in."

The colonel chewed vigorously on his pipe. "I don't have to tell you gentlemen that time is of the essence here." Stopping in his tracks, he eyed the Frenchman and stated, "Mr. Beaumont, you'll undoubtedly get your commission tomorrow and the two of you can work together until both the Holman and Dressler matters are cleared up. Are you in agreement with this?"

"Yes, sir," replied Beaumont.

Turning back to Lonegan, Harrington instructed, "In terms of priorities, if need be, get Holman first. If the Indians get their hands on modern repeater rifles— well, with things strained as they are between the

Cheyenne and the Army, it might encourage them to chance an uprising."

"Seems to me, Colonel," mused Lonegan, "if the Cheyenne are in the market for repeater rifles, somebody among them has that idea in his head already."

"Probably our skunk," put in Beaumont. "Burning Sun may be sincere when he says he wants peace, but there must be a traitor among his people who wants war. And if so, he no doubt has a good number of warriors lined up with him."

The big captain snapped his fingers. "Sure! That's it! If there's a bunch of Dog Men who want war with the whites, what better way to bring it about than to play the old chief and the Army against each other? Help a band of white men to masquerade as Cheyenne and raid white ranchers and farmers and the like. That's exactly what's happening!"

"I think we're onto it, Vint," Beaumont said excitedly. "It appears both packs of outlaws we're lookin' for are workin' with a subversive element among the Dog Men band."

Vint Lonegan toyed with the end of his mustache. "Sure has the look of it, my friend." Turning to Harrington, he said, "Maybe you ought to see Burning Sun again, sir. Tell him your thoughts on Dressler and that he may have some traitors among his Dog Men."

"I wish I could do that," murmured the colonel, "but at this point, all we have is conjecture, no proof. Throwing the traitor idea at the old boy in his present frame of mind might just touch flame to the fuse. I'm going to give you and Beaumont some time first. It would be a whole lot better if you could catch Holman and Dressler red-handed and expose the traitorous Dog Men that way." Harrington paused a few seconds and then added, "By the way, Vint. Burning Sun isn't at the main village right now."

"Oh?"

"He's got a hunting encampment set up about halfway between here and Cheyenne, right on the Blue River about ten miles north of where it flows into the North Platte. My scouts tell me there are several hundred tepees in the camp—probably the entire Hotamitanui band, including women and children."

A strange look flitted across Captain Vint Lonegan's face as he felt an old anguish rise to the surface. Then he said blithely, "Must be a lot of buffalo in that area if the Cheyenne have set up a camp that size. Sounds like they'll be there awhile."

"Scouts are reporting several huge herds," agreed the colonel. Then returning to the subject at hand, he said, "Vint, I'm counting on you and Mr. Beaumont to put a quick end to the gunrunning and eliminate the danger of arming the hostiles with such modern weapons. Just as bad, the majority of farmers, ranchers, and townspeople between here and Cheyenne are convinced that the raiders are Dog Men, and they're on the brink of uniting and launching their own attacks on various Cheyenne encampments, seeking revenge. They're blaming the Army for not stopping the raids, but they fail to understand how shorthanded of troops we are here."

"Whew!" gasped Lonegan. "Talk about the proverbial powder keg—and we're sitting on it!"

Colonel Donald Harrington's face became one of grave concern. Looking deeply into the big captain's eyes, he told him softly, "I realize this puts a tremendous burden on the shoulders of you and your friend, Vint, but you've got to stop Holman and Dressler before we have an all-out war."

Captain Vint Lonegan and William Louis Beaumont were sitting by themselves in the mess hall, eating breakfast, when Beaumont suddenly turned and stared at his companion quizzically.

Uncomfortable under his friend's intent gaze,

Lonegan nervously ran a hand through his blond hair and then asked, "Okay, what is it?"

The Frenchman laughed. "Sorry. I was just thinkin' about the bitterness in your voice last night when that Three Hands was mentioned—and the look that came over you when the colonel mentioned the Cheyenne women and children. They've been puzzlin' me ever since."

Lonegan was silent for a long moment before mumbling, "Oh, so you noticed it, eh?"

"Yep, I noticed it. Want to tell me about it?"

The captain stared down at his plate, reluctant at first to speak about his personal life. Then he sighed and said, "Well, I guess you've got a right to know, since we'll be riding together. Do you remember me telling you that the woman I loved was out of reach?"

Nodding, Beaumont replied, "Sure. I presume the lady's married to someone else and— Oh, of course! She's an Indian, isn't she? And her family doesn't want her marryin' any white man, right?"

Lonegan sighed deeply. "That's part of it. The other part is that her father has already picked out a husband for her . . . Three Hands."

"Three Hands! Burning Sun's right-hand man?" Beaumont's eyes widened. "Don't tell me your lady love is Burning Sun's daughter!"

Lonegan nodded slowly. "I'm afraid so." He smiled wryly, adding, "Just my luck, eh?"

"How did you meet?"

"Well, Little Star—that's her name—her mother, Soft Wind, was a half-breed. She wanted her daughter educated in the white man's knowledge, and she had her enrolled at a Methodist mission school in Cheyenne. About two years ago I was out on an assignment, and I happened along when two braves were escorting Little Star and Soft Wind back to their village from the school. One of the braves had just shot a big bull buffalo, wounding it, and suddenly the angered bull attacked and butted the horses, knocking all the riders to the ground. When I came upon the scene, the bull had already killed Soft Wind and one of the braves. It had wounded the second brave and was going after Little Star, but fortunately I shot and killed it in the nick of time."

Beaumont's eyes were wide with amazement. "Whew! That's some story! What happened then?"

"I took Little Star, the brave, and the bodies to the village—and I have to admit that along the way, I found myself increasingly attracted to Little Star. When we reached the village, Burning Sun, although grieved over the loss of his squaw, felt beholden to me for saving his daughter's life, and he asked me to honor him by staying for a few days. I did, and during that time Little Star and I became . . . well, very close. She admitted that she was as drawn to me as I was to her. Over the next several months, I returned to the village as often as I could, and Little Star and I both knew we had fallen in love. Eventually I asked Burning Sun for his daughter's hand in marriage, but he refused, saying she was already promised to his favorite warrior, Three Hands."

"How did Little Star take it?"

Smiling, Lonegan replied, "She showed her fiery nature. As a matter of fact, she went into a rage, for she didn't know of her father's plans. But even though she swore she would never marry Three Hands, it did no good. Burning Sun became furious and told her she was going to obey him"—Lonegan paused, looking down at his lap—"and then he ordered me to leave and never return."

The two men were quiet for a while, lost in thought. Then Beaumont asked, "Do you figure the weddin' has taken place?"

Lonegan shrugged. "I don't really know. Little Star's twenty-two by now, well past marrying age for a maiden. But her father had said something about wanting to keep her at home a while longer because her mother was dead." He sighed again. Looking around to make sure no one was listening, the captain admitted, "When we get near the Cheyenne settlement, I'm going to sneak in and try to see her."

"And if she's married to Three Hands?" the Frenchman inquired.

"I'll slip away quietly and never try to see her again," Lonegan responded gravely.

It was early afternoon when Colonel Donald Harrington sent one of his aides to find Vint Lonegan and William Louis Beaumont. The two men had been in the stables, preparing their mounts for the impending trip. They followed the corporal across the compound to the commandant's office, and when they entered, the colonel stood up and smiled in greeting.

"Ah, gentlemen, I have excellent news. Mr. Beaumont's commission has been approved."

"Great, Beau!" Lonegan exclaimed.

Harrington then told the Southerner, "Mr. Beaumont, in my wire to General Payne, I requested that you be given the same rank that you had in the Confederacy, and that has been approved. You will of course receive lieutenant's pay during the tenure of your commission."

"Thank you, sir," Beaumont responded with a smile.

Vint Lonegan then suggested, "If we leave immediately, we can get a half day's ride in before dark. Since Clete Holman was through this area a few days ago, we can probably pick up his trail easily."

Beaumont nodded his agreement. "As I told you, the sooner the better."

Harrington sent his aide out to summon another junior officer as witness, and when they returned, the colonel said to Beaumont, "We can now swear you in as a lieutenant in the United States Army. General Payne said your commission will remain in effect until I deem the assignment completed."

As soon as the swearing-in was completed, the witnesses made a quick exit. Vint Lonegan clapped a hand on the Frenchman's shoulder and advised, "Now, Lieutenant, may I remind you that I am your superior officer? You can no longer address me as Vint. You will call me sir or Captain Lonegan at all times."

Beaumont gave his friend an arch look and, shaking his head slowly, muttered, "You've gone clean out of your noggin."

Harrington laughed. "Well, Captain, I'd say you two were a perfect match. You both show a marked degree of insubordination—and shall we say a high regard for bending rules?"

"Now, Colonel . . ." Lonegan laughingly protested.

Grinning, the commandant put up his hands. "Never mind, Vint. Your methods might be slightly unorthodox at times—but they get the job done." His face sobered, and he shook Lonegan's and Beaumont's hands in turn. "Good luck, gentlemen. I hope you can put an end to this matter in short order."

Since the last report had Clete Holman and his three men heading westward, the two officers rode out of Fort McPherson in that direction. They soon ran into travelers who had seen men matching the gang's description and, guided by a series of eyewitnesses, they easily dogged Holman for a good ninety miles.

"Look's like the gunrunner's trail will be taking us close to the Cheyenne hunting camp," Vint Lonegan pointed out to his friend late in the afternoon on their third day in pursuit. "I'd say it's more and more obvious that Holman's dealing with someone in Burning Sun's band."

Eyeing the big Army man closely, Beaumont said

wryly, "I don't suppose it disappoints you that it seems that we'll end up awfully close to Little Star."

"Nope. I don't suppose it does."

At nightfall, the two Army officers made camp on the Blue River some three miles south of the Hotamitanui encampment. Soon after they had eaten, Lonegan stood up and told Beaumont he was going to sneak to the camp. "Seeing as how we're in such close proximity, it's the perfect opportunity to find out if Little Star's marriage to Three Hands has taken place—and I don't intend to pass it up."

Beaumont looked at his friend by the light of their crackling campfire and noted, "Vint, if ever I've seen a man desperately in love, I'm lookin' at him. I hope you find your woman . . . and I hope things go your way."

"Thanks."

"But you be careful, hear? I'm too tired to bail you out of trouble tonight."

Lonegan grinned and then promised, "I'll be careful. After all, I wouldn't want your first assignment as an officer of the United States Army to be escorting your commanding officer's body back for a full military funeral."

So saying, Captain Vint Lonegan strode to his horse. Climbing into the saddle, he rode hard to the north by the light of the full moon rising on the eastern horizon.

Chapter Five

A short distance beyond the west bank of the moon-dappled Blue River, a Cheyenne maiden carrying a wooden bucket lifted back the flap of the encampment's largest tepee and headed toward the water. Little Star was aptly named, for the beautiful young woman was small and finely boned—but what she lacked in size she made up for in other ways. Highly spirited, she was both deeply compassionate and fiery tempered. And although extremely feminine, Little Star was an accomplished horsewoman and a crack shot with a rifle, better at both than most of the braves in the Hotamitanui band.

As Burning Sun's daughter walked past the huge bonfire in the center of the compound and made her way toward the river, her long black hair shimmered in the glow of the flames. She was clad in a body-skimming fringed doeskin dress, which accentuated rather than hid her lovely figure. As she glided among her milling people, the appreciative eye of many a young brave followed her graceful form.

But although Little Star was a beautiful and desirable young woman, no Cheyenne young man made any attempt to win her attention. Ever since she had been promised by her father to his brave and valiant subchief, to flirt with Little Star was to flirt with death. The mighty Three Hands tolerated only the most casual friendships between his bride-to-be and the young men of the Cheyenne nation.

The comely maiden passed several men and women who were stretching buffalo hides on wooden racks, but she gave the activity only a casual glance as she weaved among the colorfully decorated tepees. Passing beyond the dwellings, she moved into the shadows of the trees crowding the riverbank when suddenly a dark, muscular form stepped from behind a tree and stood before her. Startled, she gasped; then as she focused on the man, she became angry.

"Must you sneak up on me like that?" she demanded harshly. "I do not appreciate your childish tactics!"

Three Hands moved into the moonlight, frowning. "That is no way for a man's betrothed to speak to him," he retorted.

Little Star eyed him with contempt. She despised the man and repeatedly found herself wishing she could ignore the dictates of tribal custom and disobey her father. Glaring at Three Hands, she assessed him critically. She found his shoulder-length hair hanging from the beaded headband lank and smelling foully of bear grease. The muscular Indian's thin, hooked nose reminded Little Star of a vulture's beak, and she loathed his wide, cruel mouth and cold eyes. Through clenched teeth, she spat, "I am betrothed to you only because it is my father's wish, and I will enter marriage with you under no false pretenses. I despise you, and I always will."

A fierceness showed in Three Hands's eyes. "Still clinging to the memory of Vint Lonegan, are you? You bring shame upon your family for being in love with a white man!"

Her own eyes flashing angrily, Little Star retorted, "Then my father the chief also brought shame upon our family. Have you forgotten that my mother was half white? If you feel so strongly, perhaps you would be wise to marry a pure Cheyenne rather than one of mixed blood!"

The muscular subchief gave her a wolfish grin. "Little Star is most beautiful when she is angry," he remarked, reaching for her.

The lithe young woman leapt backward out of his reach. "You are not to touch me!" she hissed. "Not until the day I am forced to become your squaw!"

Leering at her, he said, "If that is your desire, I will wait. But when we are wed, I will make you forget your beloved Vint Lonegan."

Again Little Star's eyes flashed with fire. "Never!" she exclaimed. "Now, please remove yourself from my path. I must fetch water from the river."

Just then there were sudden shouts of excitement coming from the encampment. Turning from her, Three Hands said, "I must see what is happening." He gave her a wicked smile. "But we will talk again later." Then he darted away.

Little Star moved to the bank of the river and leaned against a huge cottonwood tree, breathing heavily. A hot lump constricted her throat and tears began coursing down her cheeks. "Oh, Vint!" she sobbed softly. "I miss you, and I love you so!"

As the brokenhearted Cheyenne maiden wept, memories both sweet and bitter raced through her mind. Her heart swelled as she recalled the times they had spent together, when they had fallen in love. But the joyous feeling was quickly replaced as she relived the day her father had commanded Lonegan to leave the village and never return, warning him that if he ever tried to see Little Star again, he would die.

Little Star rolled her head against the rough bark of the big tree, picturing in her mind the grim look on her beloved's face when he told her good-bye. They both had known that if she had run away with him, Burning

Sun would have had every warrior in the Cheyenne nation on their trail, certainly resulting in Vint Lonegan's death. Vividly, she remembered watching his broad back diminish in size as he had ridden away, head bent low.

Little Star's reverie was interrupted by loud, angry voices coming from the center of the camp. Drawing a shaky breath and wiping away her tears, the maiden set down her bucket and hurried back to the compound.

Halting near the edge of the bonfire, beyond its light, she saw a number of angry braves, headed up by a Hotamitanui warrior named Hungry Wolf, tying three braves to three adjacent smaller trees at the far edge of the clearing. The rest of the camp's warriors were pressing around them, their angry voices a babel—so much so that Little Star could not understand what was being said. *What have my Cheyenne brothers done to receive such treatment?* she wondered. Moving unnoticed, she skirted the edge of the ring of firelight in order to get closer for a better view.

As Hungry Wolf and the others finished tying the three men to the trees, Little Star saw what everyone was so angry about. The captives were not Indians at all. They were white men wearing Cheyenne clothing and some kind of copper-colored paint on their skin. The paint on their faces had been smeared, exposing their pale skin. Also revealed by the firelight was the stark terror on the sweat-beaded faces of the impostors, for an incensed Hungry Wolf was promising them torture and death.

The entire village was aware of the trouble the Army had been giving their chief over raids on farms, ranches, wagon trains, and stagecoaches. They also knew Burning Sun was telling the truth when he had vehemently denied that his warriors were involved. Now the mystery was solved. Hungry Wolf's impassioned words chilled the night air as he called upon

their gods to curse the white charlatans before him—
one of whom was the raiders' leader.

The furious Hotamitanui were eager to tear the
captives limb from limb and were shouting for revenge.
Then suddenly a hush came over the crowd as the flap
of the chief's tepee was turned back, and the people
waited expectantly. The malicious face of Three Hands
appeared first; then he stepped to one side, allowing the
venerable chief to exit. Three Hands's imposing form
followed behind Burning Sun as he walked slowly toward the prisoners through a stillness broken only by
the popping of logs in the fire.

The deathly silence prevailed as the Hotamitanui
leader halted before the three captives and impassively
assessed them. Clad in beaded buckskin, Burning Sun
was regally impressive in the chief's full headdress and
the choker of four-inch bear claws circling his wrinkled
neck. Heavily beaded elk-skin moccasins adorned his
feet.

Forcing himself to meet the venerable chief's eyes,
Todd Dressler, former corporal in the United States
Army, was sorely regretting his decision to desert. He
then flicked a glance from the chief to Three Hands,
silently pleading for help—with a look that threatened
if Three Hands did not come to their aid, they would
spill the beans about the warrior's involvement.
Dressler again studied Burning Sun, but the chief's face
was an impenetrable, immobile mask as he stood glaring at the three horrified white men for a long, almost
unbearable moment.

The weighty silence was finally broken by Burning
Sun's harsh, measured growl. "White-eyes impostors
give Cheyenne bad reputation! Soldiers accuse Burning
Sun of breaking treaty! For this you die!"

"No, please!" begged Dressler, whose body was
trembling like a leaf in the wind. "Please, you can't kill
us!" He swallowed hard and then said, "Look, I'm a
soldier myself! My name's Todd Dressler, and I'm a

corporal in the United States Army . . . that is, I was. Please! We didn't mean no harm by it! We—"

The trembling man threw another quick warning look at Three Hands and then caught himself. Studying the subchief of the Dog Men band, whose hawklike face was completely impassive, Dressler suddenly realized that even if he implicated the warrior, it would be his word against Three Hands's. It did not take a genius to figure out which one of them Burning Sun would believe.

"You are leader?" Burning Sun abruptly demanded.

"Yes. Yes, sir," Dressler muttered nervously.

"How many men you have painted up to look like Cheyenne?"

Todd Dressler cleared his throat. "N-nine, sir. Uh, that is, ten, including me."

The aged chief narrowed his piercing black eyes. "Why you do this?"

Dressler's gaze automatically flicked to Three Hands again, and the warrior's countenance was fierce. Dressler looked away quickly and, drawing a shaky breath, he replied, "J-just having ourselves a little fun, your majesty. We . . . we never realized it was causing you any t-trouble."

Burning Sun's iron face remained unchanged. "Where you get Cheyenne horses, clothing, and arrows?"

Iciness drained into Todd Dressler's stomach, forming into a hard, cold knot. He could feel the flinty gaze of Three Hands boring into him though he did not take his eyes off Burning Sun. Swallowing hard, he considered his predicament. To tell the truth and expose Three Hands would undoubtedly be suicide, for the warrior would simply call him a liar and run him through with a spear to defend his honor. To say they stole the horses and other goods was possibly a hair's breadth this side of suicide. Choosing the slightly better odds, he murmured weakly, "We stole them, sir . . . uh, Chief."

Disbelief was written all over Burning Sun's weathered face. "You lie! It take plenty good thieves to sneak into Cheyenne village and steal bows, arrows, garments, and horses for ten men! Cheyenne traitor supply them!"

The word *traitor* went through the camp like a bolt of lightning. Those who knew the English word quickly translated it for the others, and almost immediately the entire tribe mutely looked around at each other. Everyone knew the Cheyenne attitude toward traitors. No white enemy ever died as slow, agonizing, and tormenting a death as did the tribesman who was guilty of treachery.

"No, Chief!" Dressler practically screamed, feeling the subchief's eyes practically burning into him. "It's the truth! We're all thieves! Outlaws! I swear on the head of my mother that I'm telling the truth!" The other two men took their cue from the corporal, joining in and assuring the angry chief that they were experts at stealing.

Burning Sun's anger seemed to reach the boiling point. "Silence!" he shouted. "My patience is gone. I will exact justice immediately!" He motioned to three warriors holding feathered spears who stood among others. As they stepped forward, Burning Sun's dark eyes blazed with fury. To Dressler he said heatedly, "You will tell me where the other seven men are, and you will name the traitor! If you refuse, each of you will die slowly with Cheyenne spears piercing your bodies in a hundred places before they are rammed through your hearts! Speak!"

Alf Kyle and Lester Nelms sagged against the ropes that held them to the trees as their knees gave way under them. Terrified, they looked at Dressler, whose face was chalky. But Dressler stalled, weighing the odds that somehow Three Hands would get them out of their mess—as opposed to killing them instantly if he were exposed as the traitor. Drawing a shuddering breath, the corporal squealed, "Please, Chief, I'm telling you the truth! We stole the horses and the other stuff! Honest!"

Swinging an arm toward Kyle, Dressler and Nelms, Burning Sun looked to the three warriors who stood ready and roared, "Use your spears!"

Dressler glared at Three Hands. He had nothing to lose now. Turning to look at the chief, he opened his mouth to speak when suddenly the subchief shouted, "Wait!" The corporal felt his whole body relax. He was certain the warrior would save their necks—somehow.

The three braves held their weapons in check and looked to Burning Sun for his order. The chief stared at his favorite warrior, his eyebrows raised in question.

Three Hands stepped in front of his chief and began speaking in English—obviously for Dressler's benefit. "May mighty Burning Sun forgive intrusion of his warrior," murmured the subchief humbly, "but Three Hands respectfully requests to speak with great chief of Hotamitanui band before white men are put to death."

The aging chieftain's eyes reflected the respect he held for the man who was soon to become his son-in-law. Slowly he raised a hand, signaling for the spears to be lowered. As the gesture was obeyed, the three captives breathed audible sighs of relief.

Burning Sun held the subchief's gaze, silently commanding him to speak, and Three Hands let his words flow quickly. "If my chief will permit his warrior to make suggestion . . ."

Burning Sun grunted, "Speak."

"Perhaps if white men are kept alive, Cheyenne will benefit."

The old chief nodded for him to continue.

"We can force them to tell where others painted up as Cheyenne are hiding. If we kill these three, others will continue to make raids, and our people will be blamed." Turning toward Dressler, he hissed, "Three Hands will torture them until they tell where other men are." Turning back to Burning Sun, he added, "If they are dead, we cannot learn where hideout is."

A grim smile tugged at the corners of the chief's mouth, and he clearly liked his warrior's line of reasoning. He nodded for Three Hands to proceed.

"When we learn location of hideout, we can bring other men here. That will end raids."

Burning Sun nodded his approval. "This is wise," he declared. "Does Three Hands have other ideas?"

"Hold them here and bring Colonel Harrington. We will make these white-eyes confess to their leader what they have done. This will make everything good with the Army again, and we will again have peace."

The old man smiled, and admiration was in his eyes. "You have shown much wisdom. It will be as you have spoken. After they confess to Colonel Harrington, then they will die." Gesturing with his chin at the three captives, he ordered, "They will stay tied to the trees. Three Hands will torture them until they give the location of their hideout."

Folding his arms with satisfaction, Three Hands looked at the captives and declared with assurance, "Chief Burning Sun may sleep well, for I will have information before sun shows its face in morning."

Burning Sun nodded and then turned and slowly walked back to his tepee. The crowd followed their chief's lead and soon dispersed.

Waiting until the only Indians within earshot were his own trusted men, Three Hands stepped in front of Dressler and, speaking low, grated, "Todd Dressler is fool! How did he get caught by Hungry Wolf?"

Dressler's face flushed, and he replied, "The three of us decided to hit a small farm by ourselves. We did well and were headed back to the hideout—but in a grove of trees, we ran head-on into Hungry Wolf and his bunch. They had us dead to rights, and there was nothing we could do."

"You gotta help us, Three Hands!" Alf Kyle pleaded hoarsely. His face was wet with tears.

The subchief eyed him coldly.

"Look, Three Hands," spoke up Dressler, "if you don't want us to implicate you, and if you want those rifles, you've gotta get us out of here! Now, old Burning Sun may not really believe us—but you can be sure he'd always be wondering somewhere in the back of his mind if maybe I was telling the truth. And besides, Clete Holman will miss us and start a search. If he finds out we're being held prisoners, you can kiss them rifles good-bye."

Three Hands pondered Dressler's words and then said, "Clete Holman wants gold too much. He will give me rifles. Besides, Burning Sun will not let you go."

"He don't need to!" gasped Nelms. "*You* let us go! Just cut these ropes and we'll do the rest!"

The subchief shook his head. "Lester Nelms is not thinking. If you run, Burning Sun will send warriors to find you. Some of them will not be my men. You will die quick!"

Nelms licked his lips nervously. "Then use your influence with the chief. Talk him into lettin' us go!"

"Burning Sun want you here to confess to bluecoat colonel. No way he can be persuaded to let you go."

"Well, that confessin' to the colonel stuff was *your* idea, Three Hands!" blurted Nelms angrily. "Why'd you go and put that in the chief's head?"

"Shut up, Les!" snapped Alf Kyle. "You're still alive, ain't you? If Three Hands hadn't brought that up, you'd be dead right now with a spear in your gut!"

Nelms then looked at Dressler. "Todd, we're still gonna die!" he whined. "You heard the chief! After we confess to Harrington, he's still gonna kill us!"

"Harrington won't let him," Dressler insisted. "We're deserters, remember? The colonel isn't gonna ride out of here and leave us to the Cheyenne. He'll take us back to Fort McPherson to be court-martialed."

"Yeah, then stand before a firin' squad!"

"Not in peacetime, you idiot!" countered Dressler. "We'll probably get ten years in prison—which sure beats dying."

"Todd Dressler is right," agreed Three Hands. "Colonel will demand he take you with him, and my chief not risk war with white man's Army to keep you for Cheyenne vengeance."

"See there," Dressler confidentally told Nelms, smiling weakly. "It's gonna be all right. You don't have to worry about dying with a Cheyenne spear through your middle."

"Here is plan," spoke up the subchief. "In morning, Three Hands will tell Chief Burning Sun that Todd Dressler feared torture so much, he willingly gave location of hideout. Three Hands will ride out of camp with band of trusted warriors and pretend to go after rest of gang. We return after many hours and tell chief Todd Dressler's men gone. Place deserted. We cannot find them."

Three Hands gave him no indication of his real plan. He had convinced Burning Sun to let the three soldiers live only because he had further use for them. Their capture had given him the perfect opportunity to carry out his scheme to take over as chief.

When Colonel Harrington came to hear their confession, Three Hands would engineer it so that only he, Burning Sun, and Harrington would meet inside Burning Sun's tepee. Prior to the meeting, Three Hands would convince the old chief that he should remain firm in his plan to kill the three deserters once they had made their confession. But Harrington would undoubtedly demand to take them with him, and Three Hands would incite an argument when the colonel demanded his men—and then Three Hands would shoot both the colonel and the chief. Before anyone had time to reach the tepee, Three Hands would take the colonel's gun and fire it into Burning Sun and then place the smoking gun near the body of the colonel. He would tell his people that the colonel had become infuriated and before Three Hands could stop him, he had shot Burning Sun, and that Three Hands had then shot the colonel in retaliation.

The warrior smiled to himself, pleased with his cleverness. Not only would this make a hero out of him to his people, but the Dog Men would then be angry enough to declare war. They could cut down whatever group of soldiers had come with the colonel and kill Dressler, Kyle, and Nelms at the same time. Burning Sun's murder would rouse the rest of the Cheyenne nation to go on the warpath. With six hundred Dog Men warriors bearing repeater rifles, the hated whites would soon be driven from Cheyenne land.

Three Hands looked at each of the captives in turn and then told Dressler, "We go now." With that, the warrior and his men walked away, soon disappearing into the night.

Looking at the men tied on either side of him, Todd Dressler said, "Boys, this isn't so bad. All we gotta do is wait it out. Thanks to our good friend Three Hands, we're gonna live!"

Les Nelms shook his head solemnly. "Todd, there's one thing you ain't thought about. We've got more than desertion to face charges for. How about the people we've killed durin' those raids?"

Sighing, Dressler responded, "I've thought about it, but I don't even want to talk about it."

"Well, if you've thought about it," retorted Kyle from the other side, "why are you so eager to face the colonel? Maybe he won't shoot us for desertion, but we'll sure enough hang for murder."

"I'm not particularly eager to face Harrington," replied Dressler, "but I'd rather take a chance on escaping from the soldiers than suffer Cheyenne justice. We have *no* chance in this situation."

"I ain't too sure we got a chance in *either* situation," Nelms mumbled glumly.

Little Star pondered the fate of the three captives as she made her way back to the rippling river. Her father would certainly kill them. These men had caused the chief much anguish, and he would not allow their transgression against the Cheyenne nation to go unpunished—or relinquish them to the Army to let their punishment be left to the white man's justice. She wondered if there would be trouble with the colonel over their pending execution.

The beautiful young maiden thought about her father's stubbornness. Once his mind was made up to something, there was nothing under heaven that could change it . . . like when he sent Vint Lonegan away, telling him never to return. Her heart grew heavy as she picked up the bucket where she had left it and stepped to the riverbank.

Reflections of the stars were dancing bits of silver on the surface of the Blue River as Little Star knelt down, dipping the bucket into the water, its mouth to the current. She felt it fill instantly, and as she lifted the bucket up, it sounded as though the river whispered her name.

Little Star paused, listening intently and then shook her head. But as she rose to her feet, she heard her name whispered again. This time she knew it was not an illusion—and it was coming from the dark shadows under the trees. Peering through the milky moonlight, she made out the form of a big, broad-shouldered man. She gasped. Setting the bucket on the ground, she glanced quickly back at the camp. When she was sure no one was watching, she dashed into the waiting arms of Vint Lonegan.

"Oh, Vint!" she breathed, embracing him. "My darling, I am so glad to see you! But . . . but you should not have come. If they catch you, my father will have you put to death!"

Lonegan's strong arms pressed her tiny body tightly against him. "My heart would not let me stay away any longer," he told her softly. "I love you, Little Star. I love you more than life itself."

Tears sprang into Little Star's eyes as she tilted her face toward his in the dappled moonlight. The captain lowered his mouth to meet hers, and their lips blended in a soft, sweet kiss.

When their mouths parted, he looked into her eyes and asked hesitantly, "Have . . . have you and Three Hands—"

"Not yet," Little Star cut in. "But the wedding is to take place in just a few days." Her body began to tremble. Laying her head against his massive chest, she clung to him with desperation. "Oh, Vint, I wish there was something we could do!"

"Me, too," he whispered. "My love for you is so deep, so strong. To live without you is to die a little each day. But we both know what would happen if I took you away with me. They would catch us—and there is no telling what kind of punishment your father would administer to you for it. I can't let that happen."

"I could take the punishment," she murmured, "but my father would torture you, and you would die a horrible death. I could not be the cause of such a thing."

There was nothing more either of them could say. It seemed that for some reason, fate had brought them together, let them fall in love and then cruelly barred them from having a life together. They clung to each other for a long moment and then kissed again.

A gust of wind ruffled the treetops overhead. Lonegan held her closer and whispered in her ear, "I will always love you, Little Star. Always."

"And I will always love you, my darling," she promised, tears now spilling down her cheeks.

"The thought of you belonging to Three Hands will be a thousand times harder to bear, now that I have held you in my arms again," he moaned.

Another long moment passed, and then he held her from him and whispered, "I must go now."

They were about to part when suddenly several dark forms separated from the shadows and lunged at Lonegan, pinning his arms. Three Hands eyed his prisoner, and in a husky voice growled, "So! The captain has violated our chief's command!"

Lonegan gave in without a struggle. "I won't resist you," he promised, "for I do not want to endanger Little Star."

Sneering, the warrior retorted, "That is too bad. I would welcome the excuse to kill you personally. As it is, I will have to settle for the pleasure of watching you endure whatever Burning Sun decrees." He gestured to his braves, commanding, "Take him to the chief."

Vint Lonegan was forced to the center of the camp and lashed to a tree just far enough away from the other three prisoners that he did not realize they were imposters. Three Hands then sent one of his men to summon the chief while Little Star stood by, trembling with fear.

Standing with his hands on his hips in front of Vint Lonegan and with a wicked gleam in his eyes, the warrior declared, "So! You thought you could have my woman!"

Lonegan merely eyed him coldly.

The subchief spat angrily in the dust and then stepped directly in front of the bound prisoner and gave his face a powerful open-handed blow, snapping Lonegan's head to the side.

Little Star suddenly pounced on Three Hands, clawing and scratching. He quickly grasped her wrists and held her so she could not move.

"Let go of me!" she demanded.

At that instant, the aging chief emerged from his

tepee, followed by Hungry Wolf. Striding up to his sub-chief, Burning Sun looked at Three Hands and commanded, "Release her."

Immediately obeying, Three Hands gave her a hard look, glaring at Little Star as she backed away rubbing her wrists.

The infuriated chief stood inches away from Vint Lonegan, his weathered face stiff with rage. Staring unwaveringly at his captive, he snarled, "Captain Vint Lonegan dares to defy Burning Sun! You were commanded many moons ago to never see my daughter again!"

Suddenly Little Star leapt in front of the chief, placing herself between him and Lonegan. "He came because he loves me, Father!" she blurted. "And I love him! If I were given my choice, I would become Vint Lonegan's squaw—not Three Hands's!"

Three Hands took a step toward Little Star, but Burning Sun laid a restraining hand against his chest. Ignoring Little Star's outburst, the chief railed at the white man, "Did I not warn you? Did I not tell you that you would die if you did this thing?"

Speaking calmly, Lonegan looked him in the eye and said fervidly, "My love for Little Star is very strong, Chief Burning Sun. It was not my desire to defy you, but I had to see her one more time."

Three Hands stiffened. Again, Burning Sun restrained him with a firm hand.

Burning Sun pointed a rigid finger at Lonegan. "You have violated Burning Sun's command! You will die at sunrise!"

"No!" screamed Little Star, flinging herself at Vint Lonegan and embracing him. "No, Father, you cannot do this! If you kill him, you must kill me, too!"

Three Hands wrenched Little Star away from the man she loved. As she struggled against his great strength, the captain shouted and strained against the rawhide thongs that held his wrists together behind the tree. Three Hands clamped the tiny maiden helplessly in his powerful grip, a triumphant sneer on his cruel mouth. "Vint Lonegan is a strong man, but he cannot break the rawhide that binds his hands. Nor can he uproot the tree that holds him fast."

"Father!" screamed the maiden. "Please! I am your flesh and blood! You cannot tear my heart out by killing the man I love! I must obey Cheyenne law by obeying you and marrying Three Hands because you have decreed it—but please, my father, I beg of you. Do not kill Vint Lonegan!"

Burning Sun turned and for a long moment looked silently at his daughter, who stood helpless in the grasp of Three Hands. His hard face softened as he beheld the beautiful young woman, her face filled with her pain and grief. "My daughter speaks with persuasion," he said softly. Looking at the subchief, he grunted, "Release her."

Three Hands obeyed, and Little Star quickly moved away from him to her father's side.

Addressing his favorite warrior, Burning Sun announced, "At sunrise, Three Hands will remove Vint Lonegan from the camp and lash him severely with bullwhip. He must learn not to defy Burning Sun. You will then release him." The chief shifted his blazing eyes to Lonegan and growled, "Little Star has convinced me to grant you your life this one time, Vint Lonegan. Now you must remain out of Little Star's life forever. If not, you will die."

With that, the chief took his daughter by the arm and escorted her back to their tepee. Little Star went reluctantly, glancing over her shoulder at the man she loved.

Waiting until Burning Sun and Little Star entered the tepee, Three Hands then stepped in front of the captain. With an evil glint in his eye, he mocked, "Have good dreams tonight, white man, for they will be your last. I will do as Burning Sun commands and take you away to be whipped—but I will not let you go. You die tomorrow morning, Vint Lonegan!"

Chapter Six

Captain Vint Lonegan leaned against the tree that held him and watched Three Hands swagger away into the shadows. The three Cheyenne who were tied near him remained silent, and he wondered what they had done to be punished in such a manner by their brothers.

The huge bonfire dwindled and became a pile of red embers. Soon all was quiet across the camp, except for the gurgling of the nearby river and the chirping of countless crickets. Presently Lonegan heard someone weeping from across the compound, and as he listened, he realized it was Little Star.

Lonegan lifted his eyes toward the star-studded sky, and bitter questions assaulted his mind. Why did things have to be this way? Why was life so unfair? Why had he and Little Star been allowed to meet and fall in love, only to be torn apart by something over which neither of them had control? Why would the lovely maiden be forced to marry a man she despised?

His thoughts were interrupted by the whispering among his fellow captives. He turned and looked at them and, giving in to his curiosity, he asked, "What is it that you braves have done?"

"We're not braves, Captain," the man in the middle replied.

Before another word was spoken, Lonegan had it figured out. These were three of the white raiders who had been impersonating Cheyenne—and obviously the Indians had caught them in the act.

The same man went on, "See, we're Army deserters, from Fort McPherson. We knew you the minute they dragged you in here. We've seen you at the fort. My name's Todd Dressler. That one's Alf Kyle, and this'n over here is Les Nelms. We just talked it over and figure it won't do no harm to tell you, seeing as how we're gonna be confessing everything to Colonel Harrington."

Not letting on that he had been assigned to track them down, Captain Vint Lonegan listened intently as they spilled it all. It was as if confessing it to him would make it easier to face the colonel. Lonegan was not suprised to learn of their connection with Clete Holman, the scheme being to supply six hundred Spencer .44 caliber repeater rifles to a dissident group of Cheyenne who wanted to wage war against the whites. But when Lonegan asked the identity of the Cheyenne warrior who was leading the traitors, they refused to divulge it to him, saying it would mean their instant death if he found out.

Dressler then told Lonegan that Three Hands was going to take a band of Dog Men and go after the rest of the gang in the morning. The captain knew this would stop the raids—but Clete Holman would still be free to deliver the weapons.

Lonegan cursed the rawhide thongs that held him captive. Then he thought of William Louis Beaumont. Certainly Beaumont would know something was wrong when Lonegan did not return to their camp by midnight—unless, of course, he was asleep and stayed that way until morning. Not that the Southerner could do anything about the situation, anyway. He was only one man, and there were more than five hundred warriors in this place. Maybe as many as six hundred. Even if he were foolhardy enough to try a rescue, it would be impossible.

Time passed, and the big man shifted his position. Looking up, he was amazed to see that the moon had completely passed from view. He swung his eyes to the east and saw a faint hint of gray on the horizon. A cold chill slithered down Lonegan's spine. It would soon be dawn.

Little Star stared up through the smoke hole at the top of the tepee, watching the sky lighten. She had spent a sleepless night, weeping until no more tears could be shed—both at the prospect of never again seeing the man she loved and knowing he would suffer a brutal beating at his enemy's hands.

Suddenly she heard a rustling sound, and she turned her head to see her father pushing back the flap and stepping outside. She sat up, a cold dread washing through her body. Vint Lonegan had come back into her life for a fleeting few moments, and now she would never see him again. "Oh, my love," she whispered softly. "If I could only see you one more time."

She crawled to the opening and lifted the flap a few inches, peering through. Her father and Three Hands, both wearing their full headdresses, were standing several feet away, talking quietly. She heard the subchief tell Burning Sun that Todd Dressler's fear of torture had quickly produced the location of the hideout.

The chief smiled humorlessly. "Good," he grunted. "Did Todd Dressler fear torture enough to also reveal the name of the traitor who has provided him with Cheyenne horses and equipment?"

There was a brief pause, and Little Star thought there was a bit of trepidation in his voice as Three Hands replied, "I did not press for this, great chief. These three who are the gang leaders fear the traitor more than they fear torture, and they would not reveal his identity. It is best to capture the rest of Todd

Dressler's gang. Some men are weaker than others. No doubt greater numbers will make it more likely to find a weak man. We will have our answer quickly."

Burning Sun nodded tightly. "All of them will die after exposing the traitor and confessing to Colonel Harrington." The old chief paused a brief moment and then added, "I have made another decision. You and Little Star will be married tonight. I will inform my daughter of this when Vint Lonegan has been taken from camp. Once you and Little Star are joined, she will forget the white man to whom she had pledged her heart."

Inside the tepee, Little Star felt faint. Throwing her hands to her face, she shook her head, moaning repeatedly, "No! No! No!"

Vint Lonegan's guts clenched when he saw Three Hands and several warriors coming toward him. They had found his horse, and one brave was leading it behind the group.

Reaching him, two of the warriors untied his hands from the tree while the subchief eyed the captain malevolently. Three Hands smiled devilishly, saying wryly, "Do not worry about Little Star, white-eyes soldier. She will be in good hands."

When Lonegan felt his wrists freed, the temptation became too great. Though his shoulders and arms were painfully sore and stiff, he pulled away from the tree and, without warning, sent a fist smashing into Three Hands's jaw. The impact of the blow snapped the Indian's head back violently and sent him reeling. Losing his footing, he landed flat on his back.

Immediately more than a dozen warriors were on Lonegan. They pulled him to the ground and pinned his face in the dirt while the thongs were once again laced around his wrists. Then he was hoisted into his saddle with his hands tied behind his back. As his ankles were being lashed together under the horse's belly with a rope, Three Hands sat up, shaking his head. He gave Lonegan a look of pure hatred, and it was obvious that he could barely control his fury.

The crowd that had been watching suddenly parted, and Chief Burning Sun came forward. Three Hands gained his feet and looked at the chief.

Burning Sun momentarily stood silently, his arms folded across his broad chest. Then his deep voice rang out. "Three Hands will take Vint Lonegan now and administer the whip to his back. Release him as I have commanded and then hasten to the hideout of Todd Dressler's gang and bring them here at once. When they are in my presence, Colonel Donald Harrington will be summoned. Go."

Forty warriors, armed with knives, spears, hatchets, and rifles, swung onto their mounts. Three Hands's horse was brought to him and, taking hold of the reins of Vint Lonegan's horse, the subchief quickly jumped astride his pinto. A bullwhip was then handed to the subchief by the same brave who had brought his horse.

Just as the procession was about to head out, Little Star bolted from her tepee and dashed toward Lonegan's horse. In desperation, she grabbed hold of the captain's left leg. "Please, Father!" she screamed. "I beg of you not to have him whipped by Three Hands!"

Burning Sun glared at his daughter and then barked a command for two braves to remove her and take her back to the big tepee. "You disgrace yourself, daughter!" he said angrily.

Trussed up and helpless to do anything, rage ran through Vint Lonegan like molten fire as the two braves stepped forward to subdue the determined maiden. She fought them, resisting as best she could, but their strength easily overpowered her. As Little Star was dragged away, she cried out, "I love you, Vint! I love you!"

"And I love you, Little Star!" Lonegan called back. "I always will!"

Jerking the reins so sharply that Vint Lonegan's body was snapped backward, Three Hands started the procession out of the encampment.

For the next half hour the column of Hotamitanui Cheyenne braves led by the ferocious Three Hands moved silently over the rolling prairie. Spring breezes skipped across the sunlit land, twisting the foot-high grass in capricious waves of green. Soon the riders reached a broad, shallow valley in the middle of which was a thick clump of cottonwood trees with a small creek running through it.

Speaking over his shoulder, Three Hands pointed ahead at the grove of trees and ordered, "We will stop there."

Vint Lonegan wondered what the subchief had in mind. Whatever it was, Lonegan knew it would be horrible and agonizing before death released him.

Moments later, the Dog Men reined in and dismounted at the edge of the dense stand of trees. Lonegan was left on his horse while Three Hands gave instructions to two braves who carried hatchets. The two men immediately began chopping thin branches from the surrounding trees until they had nine in all. The branches were then cut into two-foot lengths and driven halfway into the ground, in three rows of three, with each stake six inches apart, near the base of a massive cottonwood. Directly over the stakes, twenty feet off the ground, was the thick bottom limb of the tree. With their knives, the two braves began whittling the tips of the stakes, shaping them to razor-sharp points.

Vint Lonegan shuddered as a cold shiver danced down his spine. He had heard of this form of Cheyenne justice, designed to first produce horrible mental torture before the victim died an excruciatingly painful death. Lonegan would be hoisted on a rope above the sharp stakes, positioned facedown so he would be

forced to look at the spears beneath him. Then a few
strands of the rope would be cut, and the pressure of his
weight against the remaining strands would cause them
to slowly break one at a time. He would hang there,
hearing and feeling the thin strands snapping, until he
finally plunged to the stakes and was impaled. If he was
lucky, one of the stakes would pierce his heart and he
would die quickly. If he was not lucky . . .

While the two braves whittled away, Three Hands
talked with his warriors, and Lonegan overheard the
subchief explain his plans. He told them that Colonel
Harrington was to be summoned to hear the confessions of the deserters, but Three Hands planned to use
the meeting to kill Colonel Harrington and Burning
Sun and then take over leadership of the Hotamitanui
Cheyenne.

The treacherous subchief told his men that the rest
of the deserters—who were waiting at a hideout—
would be used to help Holman get the rifles onto a small
island in the North Platte River, where Three Hands
and his men would pick them up. As soon as they had
the rifles, Holman and the rest of the deserters would
die.

One of the warriors asked Three Hands if he would
murder Burning Sun and the colonel before the rifles
were in hand, and the subchief answered, "No. I will
make no move that would stir up trouble with the Army
until we have the weapons. I will see to it that the
runners who go for the colonel are my trusted braves.
They can delay the bluecoat's arrival until the rifles
have been delivered."

Another asked, "What if somehow your plan for
killing Burning Sun is thwarted?"

The traitor replied coolly, "Then I will come up
with another way to murder Burning Sun and let the
whites take the blame. It must appear that the whites
have done it so as to incite the rest of the Dog Men to
war—and this will cause the other bands in the Chey-

enne nation to join us. Every white-eyes outpost on Cheyenne land will be wiped out, and soon we will be rid of all the hated invaders."

While the whoops and cheers of the dissident warriors rang in his ears, Vint Lonegan felt his blood run cold. It made him sick that Little Star would unknowingly be the squaw of the traitorous scum who had murdered her father. He cursed the bonds that held him, thinking that nothing would give him greater pleasure than to tear Three Hands apart with his bare hands.

Suddenly the two warriors fashioning the stakes announced that they were finished. Three Hands grinned gleefully and swaggered over to examine their handiwork. He bent down and touched the tip of each stake with a forefinger and, satisfied that they all were sharp enough, he turned to his warriors and ordered, "Take Vint Lonegan from his horse."

Untying Lonegan's ankles from under the horse's belly, four Dog Men wrenched him from the horse's back, slamming him hard to the ground. With his hands still tied behind his back, the captain awkwardly got to his knees and looked up to see Three Hands—a hellish hatred burning in his eyes—uncoiling the bullwhip. Lonegan ducked his head as the whip hissed and lashed him across the neck and shoulders.

The warriors cheered their leader on as he cracked the whip repeatedly while laughing with fiendish glee. Lonegan rolled on the ground, trying to avoid the cutting tip of the whip, but Three Hands was too skillful and continually cut him. Determination welled up within Lonegan, and while the whip lashed him, the big man gained his feet and bolted forward, violently driving his head into Three Hands's midsection. The impact of Lonegan's two hundred and twenty muscular pounds knocked the Indian from his feet and the breath from his lungs. He rolled about, gasping hard for air and moaning in pain.

A half-dozen warriors seized Vint Lonegan and

held him while Three Hands stood up, clutching his stomach. Flushed with rage, the traitor's marblelike eyes glared murderously at the captain as he declared, "It is time for you to die, white eyes!"

Lonegan was dragged over to the massive cottonwood tree, and the wrenching made the stinging, bleeding welts on his back, neck, and shoulders even more excruciatingly painful. Blood trickled from his left cheekbone, mingling with his sweat, and it ran into the corner of his mouth as he was flung to the ground next to the stakes.

A long rope was slung over the thick limb above the stakes. With one end of the rope, the captain was trussed underneath his arms and around his waist; then the rope was looped around his ankles, bending them over his back. Six Dog Men grasped the other end of the rope and hoisted Lonegan up until he dangled horizontally above the deadly stakes. The other end of the rope was then secured to the trunk of the tree.

Vint Lonegan eyed the nine finely honed points directly below him, and they seemed to be reaching up at him hungrily. He glanced at Three Hands, who was standing with a malicious leer on his dark face. Turning to one of the braves, the subchief commanded, "Dark Cloud, climb up on the limb and cut halfway through the rope. I do not want Vint Lonegan to die *too* soon— but I also do not want him to live much longer."

Dark Cloud obediently climbed the tree with a knife between his teeth. Balancing on the limb, he began sawing through the braided rope.

Lonegan broke into a cold sweat as he felt the rope split and give under Dark Cloud's knife. After examining his work and satisfied that just the right amount of rope was left intact, the warrior shinnied down the tree. The big captain's bulk pulled hard against the remaining strands, and one by one they began to pop, split, and unravel.

Three Hands stood below, hands on hips, and

looked up into Lonegan's face. Throwing his head back, he laughed wickedly and mocked, "I could not allow my white-eyes enemy to die without letting him first stare into the face of death for a brief time!"

Then turning to Dark Cloud, Three Hands ordered, "Dark Cloud, you, Broken Nose, and Short Arrow will remain here until the captain falls. Though it would give me great pleasure to watch my enemy die, I must take the others and go to the hideout to see if there is word from Clete Holman. When Lonegan is dead, find a gully for his body and leave it for the animals and vultures to devour. Then return to camp and tell Burning Sun that Three Hands whipped Vint Lonegan so severely, you three had to stay with him until he was able to ride."

Dark Cloud nodded obediently.

Turning back to Lonegan, Three Hands gave his enemy a malevolent smile and said, "Oh, yes, white-eyes lover of Little Star, I almost forgot to tell you. Chief Burning Sun has set the wedding for tonight. Too bad you will not be able to attend the festivities!"

Three Hands was laughing hard as he commanded his warriors to mount up, and then he swung onto his own pinto. Looking one last time at Lonegan, he laughed again and rode away, followed by his warriors.

As the band of Dog Men galloped away, the captain eyed the lethal points that waited below. Although the thunder of the pintos galloping away blanketed all other sounds, Lonegan imagined he could clearly hear the soft, distinct popping of the rope strands.

Dark Cloud, Broken Nose, and Short Arrow sat down, leaning against nearby trees, and waited for the rope to give way. It was clear from their faces that they eagerly anticipated the white man's plunge to his death.

Sweat running into the welts on Vint Lonegan's face caused them to sting horribly, and he turned his face to the side. From his high position, he suddenly caught movement behind the three Indians in the tall grass, and then he made out the figure of a man crawling toward them. A few more seconds passed and the figure materialized into William Louis Beaumont. Lonegan's heart quickened pace.

It seemed unnaturally quiet. The pinging sound of the disintegrating rope sounded like rifle shots in Lonegan's ears, and he had the urge to scream at Beaumont and tell him to hurry. But to call to him would eliminate the element of surprise, and being outnumbered three to one, the Frenchman needed that advantage. He would have to take out all three Dog Men without using his gun, for a shot could bring Three Hands and the others back in a hurry.

A gust of wind suddenly swayed Vint Lonegan's huge frame, and the movement made the rope twist, breaking more strands. He felt his heart leap to his throat as the rope gave some more. Down below, the three braves assessed his ever-worsening predicament and laughed.

Abruptly, Dark Cloud noticed his pinto rubbing its neck on a feathered lance that the Indian had stuck in the ground when he dismounted. The lance was bending from the weight, close to breaking, and the Indian leapt to his feet to get his spear out of the animal's way. Beaumont reached the mottled shadows of the trees just as the brave moved the lance and drove it into the ground. Seeing the white man, Dark Cloud uttered a harsh word in his own language and pulled his knife. The other two braves became alert and started scrambling to their feet.

Moving quickly, Beaumont reached down and threw a handful of dirt in Dark Cloud's face, and the Indian sputtered and clawed at his eyes. The Frenchman then chopped him with a hard blow to the jaw, and he went down. In the same instant, the Southerner seized the lance and pulled it from the sod, then faced the two warriors who were coming at him with their knives flashing. Beaumont danced about to throw them off balance as they came on the run, and they staggered a bit, trying to stay with him. Timing his move perfectly, the lithe Frenchman hurled the lance, burying it in the chest of one of the braves. The Indian screamed, dropped his knife, and fell backward, gripping the lance with both hands.

The other brave shrieked and lunged at Beaumont, knife poised. Dodging him, the Frenchman picked up the dead Indian's knife. The brave pivoted and came at the white man, ready to kill, and he and Beaumont collided, falling to the ground and rolling over and over, knife blades seeking flesh.

Watching his friend fighting for his own life, Vint Lonegan's heart beat wildly, feeling the rope give some more as the remaining strands continued to break. He prayed that somehow Beaumont would triumph quickly, for any second he would fall to his death.

The Frenchman and the Indian got to their feet, and the agile brave threw a heel behind Beaumont's foot, tripping him. The brave raised his knife, ready for the kill, but the Southerner adeptly kicked the Cheyenne in the groin. While the Indian was doubled over in pain, Beaumont's hand came up quickly and drove the knife into the man's throat.

Vint Lonegan swallowed hard, listening to the rope strands breaking more rapidly and promising certain death. Shifting his gaze from the stakes, he saw Dark Cloud, his vision finally clear, dashing toward the Frenchman from behind. "Beau!" the captain shouted. "Behind you!"

Beaumont was just rising to his feet with the bloody knife in his hand. He wheeled in time to avert the deadly swing of Dark Cloud's blade. Pure hatred was evident in the Indian's watering eyes as he came at the white man again. The battle-wise Southerner leapt at the Indian, swinging the bloody knife in his hand.

Dark Cloud took a step back and stumbled slightly.

Beaumont lunged again with his knife, throwing himself onto his adversary and shoving him to the ground as he drove the blade into Dark Cloud's stomach. Leaving the dying man writhing in agony on the ground, the Southerner ran over to the big cottonwood tree to release Vint Lonegan.

Suddenly from overhead Lonegan shouted, "Beau!"

The Frenchman flicked a glance upward. The last of the rope strands were breaking above his friend's dangling body. He frantically began twisting the stakes out of the ground, but there was not sufficient time to do so. His face reflecting his anquished desperation, he ran back a few steps, then kicked with all his might at the stakes, managing to flatten them just as Vint Lonegan fell.

Chapter Seven

Little Star sat solemnly in the big tepee at the Hotamitanui camp, sickened at the prospect of becoming Three Hands's squaw that evening and determined to get away so the wedding could not take place. But it would not be easy. Knowing his daughter was deeply disturbed over the impending marriage and also knowing the spirited young woman might well try to go to Lonegan, Burning Sun had stationed two braves outside the tepee as a precaution. Looking toward the flap, Little Star could see their shadows cast against the tepee by the early morning sun.

Deciding she had to try, the maiden hurried to the rear of the tepee and began loosening the cords that held it to the stakes. When she had slackened the buffalo hide enough to squeeze her small frame underneath, she crawled through the opening and then dashed for the corral, threading her way among the brightly colored tepees. But as she reached the rope corral, the two guards spotted her and gave a shout and then came on the run. Before Little Star could leap onto her pinto and gallop off, the braves had her in their grasp.

"Let me go!" she screamed.

"We cannot, Little Star," said one. "Your father has ordered us to keep you in the camp."

Fighting them all the way, Little Star dug her heels in the dirt as they dragged her back to the tepee. Burning Sun was waiting for them, his arms folded over his chest, and his stern eyes bored into her. "My daughter has shamed her father!" the chief said scornfully. "You will obediently remain in the tepee until it is time to be joined with Three Hands!"

Little Star did not respond. Disconsolate, she entered the tepee and pulled the flap closed. She heard her father assigning two additional braves to retie the cords and remain posted at the rear of the tepee, ensuring that she would not try to escape again.

The Indian maiden's heart felt as if it would wrench itself from her breast, and her tears seemed to burn her cheeks. She ached to be with the man she loved and worried that the repugnant Three Hands had tormented him with his whip.

The angered and embittered young woman paced back and forth in the tepee like a caged animal, dreading what lay ahead of her. Later that afternoon, four squaws would enter the tepee to help the bride dress for the ceremony and fix her hair. She would then wait for darkness to fall and the fire dance would begin, with the thunder of the drums filling the camp. When Burning Sun felt the fire dance had gone on long enough, he would come to the tepee and escort her to the center of the compound, where Three Hands would be waiting near the huge fire. With great pomp and ritual, the Hotamitanui chief would present Little Star to his favorite warrior and then conduct the marriage ceremony.

Little Star shuddered as she pictured the scene—even more so when she thought of being alone with Three Hands in his tepee. Her pacing stopped, and she threw her hands to her face and wept.

* * *

Beneath the cottonwoods on the prairie, recovering from the ordeal, Captain Vint Lonegan listened as Lieutenant William Louis Beaumont explained how he happened to come upon him in the nick of time.

When Beaumont had awakened at first light and found that the captain had not returned, he had headed for the Cheyenne camp, assuming something had happened. He had reached the encampment just as the band of Dog Men were leading Lonegan away and, staying far enough behind to remain out of sight, he had followed them. The Southerner then had had to wait for just the right moment until he could come in and attempt the rescue.

Lonegan shook his head in amazement. "That sure was some commendable fighting you did, Beau. Not too many people would have come out on top with three-to-one odds—especially against Cheyenne warriors." He paused and grinned, adding, "I guess I owe you double now." He then told the Frenchman what he had learned concerning Three Hands, Clete Holman, and Todd Dressler—including the shipment of six hundred repeater rifles and the planned murder of Burning Sun. He also told him about the marriage that was to take place that evening between Little Star and Three Hands.

William Louis Beaumont was momentarily stunned. Then he swore angrily and declared, "Vint, where do we begin? We've got to prevent the meeting between Colonel Harrington and Burning Sun from happenin' 'cause there'll be bloodshed for sure if the chief refuses to turn over those three deserters to him. We've got to stop that snake-eyed traitor before he kills the chief and soaks this prairie with blood—and we've got to stop that weddin'!"

"No doubt about it, we've got our hands full," agreed Lonegan. "The best way to keep Three Hands from getting those rifles is by finding the hideout where the rest of Dressler's men are waiting. As for the rest of it, I've got a plan."

"Let's hear it."

"We've got to sneak into the Hotamitanui camp and come out with five people."

Beaumont's eyes bulged. "Oh, is that all? Us and what army?"

"Just us."

Pulling the end of his mustache, the Frenchman asked wryly, "Captain Lonegan, sir, just how in the name of Ulysses S. Grant are we going to accomplish this feat?" A quizzical look came over his face, and he continued, "And by the way, *what* five people?"

"We've got to get Little Star out before the wedding takes place."

"Granted."

"We take Dressler and his two pals so they can lead us to the hideout—that'll be our biggest step toward plugging up the delivery of those repeaters to Three Hands."

"Good thinking. That's four. Who's number five?"

"Three Hands."

Beaumont's face lit up. "Good! We can blow his stinkin' head off!"

"I'm afraid not," Lonegan quippped, grinning. "Here's how it'll work."

The captain explained that he knew a great deal about Cheyenne weddings, so he knew where the principals would be before and during the rite. The best time to free Little Star would be when she was being escorted by her father from the tepee to the center of the compound where the ceremony would take place.

Beaumont would have to dash in and get a headlock on Three Hands's neck, putting a gun to his head. At the same time, Lonegan would free the three white captives. The captain was certain that Burning Sun would do nothing to endanger his daughter or his favorite warrior, but to ensure it, Lonegan would promise

Burning Sun that Three Hands would not be harmed if no one followed them. If they were followed, Three Hands would be killed.

"Why not just tell Burning Sun that his fair-haired boy—in a manner of speakin'—is planning to kill him?"

Lonegan grimaced. "Because he'd never believe us. Besides, if he *did* believe us, we'd die on the spot because he wouldn't care if anything happened to Three Hands and we'd be guilty of kidnapping his daughter and the three soldiers. No, I'm afraid we'll just have to try it this way, and when we're a safe distance from the camp, we'll release Three Hands—even though I'd like to put a bullet between his eyes."

"Guess Burning Sun'll have to find out some other time," observed the Frenchman.

"Yeah. The main thing right now is to stop the wedding and the delivery of those rifles. Burning Sun is in no danger of being murdered by Three Hands until the rat has the weapons. We'll lock up the rifles, *then* set a trap for the traitor."

The sun was throwing lengthy shadows across the Hotamitanui camp when four squaws emerged from the big tepee. Inside, her hair now braided and beaded for the wedding and dressed in a fringed doeskin dress and beaded moccasins, Little Star paced the floor, wringing her hands.

Her anxious pacing did not last long before there was a rustling at the flap and Burning Sun appeared. He stepped in, dropped the flap into place, and looked intently at his daughter, studying her harried face. Wordlessly, he sat down cross-legged on a woven rug and folded his arms over his chest, his face expressionless.

After a moment's hesitation, Little Star knelt on the rug across from her father, sitting on her haunches, and then slowly lifted her gaze to his stoical face. The silence was thick as Burning Sun regarded his daughter with piercing eyes. Finally he told her, "My daughter should be happy on her wedding day."

Her face grim, Little Star spoke tonelessly. "Your daughter will never be happy again. You have sent away forever the man I love."

"Does my daughter hold no respect for her father? She is a young and foolish child while I, with the wisdom that age and experience impart, know what is best for her. Three Hands is the bravest and mightiest of the Dog Men warriors, my daughter. He will one day be Hotamitanui chief. It will bring much honor to Little Star to be his squaw."

The maiden wanted to scream at him, tell him he was being stubborn and unfair and that she refused to marry Three Hands. But she could not, and so she held her peace. Any words that she might utter would change nothing.

The two of them sat silently, gauging each other. Then suddenly the imposing silence was disrupted by the sound of horses thundering into the encampment. Without a further word, the aging chief stood up and stepped out into the late afternoon sun, letting the flap fall back into place. Little Star was rising to her feet when she heard a young boy in the camp call out the name of Three Hands. Her heart suddenly felt like cold lead. The vile subchief had returned. She stepped to the side of the tepee and listened intently, anxious to hear about Vint Lonegan.

Leaving his pinto for the warriors to take to the corral, Three Hands walked toward Burning Sun. As he walked, the subchief looked around for the three braves he had left with Lonegan, but there was no sign of them. He wanted confirmation that Lonegan had been impaled on the stakes and that his body was now lying in a gully somewhere on the plains. Three Hands was nettled at the absence of Dark Cloud, Broken Nose, and Short Arrow, but no matter. He would tell the chief that

Vint Lonegan had been whipped severely and set free —just what Burning Sun wanted to hear.

Facing the chief, the lie came easily from Three Hands's mouth. He then told Burning Sun that Dressler's hideout had been found, but it had been deserted and the other men had been nowhere to be found.

Anger flared in the old chief's weathered face. Gritting his teeth, he declared, "At the rising of the sun, riders will be sent to Fort McPherson to bring Colonel Donald Harrington."

Three Hands nodded. "It will be so, my chief."

Burning Sun, gazing sternly at the three men still tied to the trees near the center of the compound, then said to Three Hands, "Because of your wedding tonight, we will wait until morning to torture the truth out of our prisoners. While we wait for the white-eyes colonel to arrive, they will tell us who the traitor is. Then we will impose our justice upon him, and the evil Cheyenne serpent will wish he had never been born!"

The subchief's heart skipped a beat. He would have to think of some way to divert the old man from this endeavor. But then he reminded himself that the men at the hideout had informed him the wagon train was a few days ahead of schedule, and Clete Holman already had eight crates of rifles and several boxes of cartridges stashed on the island. The last shipment would be arriving at the stage office in Oshkosh today—which meant the Dog Men would have the repeater rifles in their hands before Colonel Donald Harrington could reach the camp.

Interrupting the traitor's reverie, the chief then announced, "When the three captives have made their confessions to the colonel, they will die!"

Nodding his agreement, Three Hands inquired, "What will my chief do if Colonel Donald Harrington demands to take the prisoners with him?"

Burning Sun snorted and replied, "There is noth-

ing the colonel can do. He will be greatly outnumbered.
Even if he should bring every soldier from his fort, the
Hotamitanui warriors are far too many. The colonel
would be a fool to wage war in our camp." Shaking his
head fiercely, the chief added, "These impostors have
committed a grievous crime against our people. They
must suffer Cheyenne justice."

That same afternoon, gunrunner Clete Holman
and his three men stood nervously beside their wagon a
few yards from the Wells Fargo office in Oshkosh, Nebraska, waiting for the stagecoach. The coach bore a
shipment of rifles and ammunition, the last of three that
had been loaded by the wagonmaster in North Platte on
the next three stagecoaches heading west. Holman and
his men had already picked up the first two shipments
and stashed them on the island in the North Platte
River; now they were anxiously awaiting the last shipment, due any minute.

A serious complication had just developed, however. A squad of twenty-five cavalrymen, on patrol from
Fort McPherson, had ridden into town, and Holman
and three of his men watched as the troopers dismounted to rest in the shade of some huge cottonwood
trees directly across the street. Though the wooden
crates on the stagecoach would be marked TOOLS, Holman was afraid to unload them and place them in his
wagon with the soldiers watching. Since the Army
knew rifles were being smuggled to the Indians in the
area, they might be suspicious.

The gunrunner took off his hat and wiped the sweat
from his brow as Harley Carter asked in a low voice,
"Clete, what're we gonna do?"

Holman knew the stage's final destination was
Scottsbluff and would stop only briefly in Oshkosh before pushing on. Its next scheduled stop would be in
Lisco, some sixteen miles farther west. Placing his hat
back on his head, Holman cast a wary eye across the

street and replied, "When the stage gets here, I'll find a way to tell the driver that we'll meet him about four miles out of town, where the road takes that slight bend northward. There won't be any nosy bluecoats out there."

Mickey Wilson scratched his head and queried, "How come the shotgunners on these runs ain't in on what's goin' on?"

"Money," replied Holman drily. "See, we have to pay off the agents and the drivers to smuggle the guns in—and there ain't no sense payin' anybody else."

Even as Holman was speaking, the North Platte stage appeared at the east end of town. The men in blue resting across the street looked toward the sound of the rumbling hooves and rattling coach. Two well-dressed businessmen stepped out of the Wells Fargo office, carrying small suitcases, and immediately behind them came the agent, ready to meet the stage. The agent threw a furtive glance from the soldiers to Clete Holman, obviously concerned about their presence, but the gunrunner gave him a look that said everything was in control. Looking relieved, the agent then put his attention on the stage as it rolled up in a cloud of dust.

The young shotgunner hurried down and opened the door of the stage. Smiling at the two lovely young women inside the coach, Billy Pine suggested, "May as well get out and stretch your legs, ladies. But you only have about ten minutes, and then we'll be rollin' again."

Offering his hand, the shotgunner helped the blonde out first, and the brunette followed. The two businessmen who were waiting to board eyed the young women appreciatively. The young women smiled at the two well-dressed men and then walked into the stage office to refresh themselves.

While a fresh team of horses was being hitched to the coach by the agent and the shotgunner, Clete Holman casually approached the middle-aged driver and spoke to him softly, telling him of the change in plans.

Suddenly the two officers in charge of the troop across the street stood up and started toward the stagecoach. Seeing them, Holman hurried his words to the driver and then headed for the wagon, where he and his men watched and listened nervously as the officers approached the driver. But the officers merely warned the driver that a large band of hostile Oglala Sioux were somewhere in the area, and then they returned to their men across the street. Sighing with relief, Holman and his men piled into their wagon and headed west out of town.

Emerging from the stage office, the two young women were informed by their driver that there were hostiles in the area. "Maybe you oughtta wait a couple o' days till the next stage comes through. Let them Indians move on outta the area."

The women looked at each other and then Becky Sue Moore smiled politely and said, "Thank you for your concern, Mr. Benson, but we'll continue on with you."

Shrugging, he climbed to the top of the box while Billy Pine helped the ladies back into the coach. The two businessmen then stepped in behind them.

As the stage rolled out of Oshkosh, the new passengers introduced themselves as Arnold Quayle and Henry Smith. Then Quayle reached under his coat and removed a small-caliber gun from a shoulder holster. Turning to his companion, he suggested, "If what that officer said is true about the Sioux, I'd better make sure this is fully loaded—just in case."

"Good idea," Smith agreed. "It isn't for nothing that it's become the custom even for us businessmen to wear arms when we travel anywhere west of the Mississippi." He looked across at the two young women and smiled. "Hope we haven't alarmed you ladies."

Becky Sue smiled. "No, quite the contrary. It's comforting to know you gentlemen are able to protect us, in case of trouble." She then introduced herself and her sister, explaining that they had spent a few days with old friends in North Platte before continuing on to Scottsbluff to attend a wedding.

"A bit young to be traveling by yourselves, aren't you, ladies?" asked Quayle.

"I'm eighteen," Becky Sue replied somewhat defensively.

"And I'm sixteen," spoke up Patty. "Our mother was married when she was my age."

"Pardon me," Quayle responded dryly, elbowing his friend.

As the coach swayed and rocked, Becky Sue looked out the window to the south. She could see the North Platte River wending its way across the prairie, looking like a ribbon of gold as it reflected the light of the lowering sun.

It seemed the coach had hardly gotten started when it began to slow down. The passengers looked at each other quizzically, then Henry Smith stuck his head out the window to see what was going on. "Four men and a wagon are waiting beside the road up ahead," he informed the others. Squinting, he added, "Funny."

"What's funny?" asked Quayle.

"I'm sure those same four men were standing around that same wagon by the stage office."

Arnold Quayle leaned out and looked and then remarked, "You're right. They're the same men."

"Are they robbers?" gasped Patty.

"Don't seem to be, Miss Moore," replied Quayle.

Up in the box, Billy Pine looked questioningly at the driver as they slowed down and asked, "What's goin' on, Harry? Who are these guys?"

"Farmers," Benson answered levelly. "They're pickin' up these tools we've been haulin' since North Platte."

"I saw them back in town," remarked the shotgunner. "Why didn't they take the tools off back there?"

"Don't ask questions, kid," warned Benson stiffly. "They'll take the crates off, and we'll be on our way."

A worried look settled onto young Pine's face.

When the stage came to a dusty halt, Harry Benson started to climb down, ordering, "You stay up here, kid. This'll only take a couple minutes."

The wagon drew up beside the coach as Arnold Quayle stepped outside, with Henry Smith following. While two of Holman's men climbed up to the luggage rack and began untying the ropes that held the four wooden crates, the gunrunner and his other crony stood in the bed of the wagon, waiting to take the boxes.

The two businessmen stood watching, but as the third crate was being transferred. Arnold Quayle suddenly asked suspiciously, "What's going on here, fellas? I saw you four in town. Why didn't you unload these tools back there?"

Reaching out to take his corner of the crate, Clete Holman gave Quayle an annoyed look and snapped, "Mind your own business, mister!"

Before the businessman could respond, Holman's fingers slipped and the crate tilted. The sudden shift of weight took him by surprise and the crate got away from him. It slipped to the ground and split open, dumping its contents.

"Rifles!" exclaimed Henry Smith to his traveling companion. "I know what these guys are doing! They're smuggling rifles to the Indians!"

The men immediately went for their guns, and there was a sudden eruption of gunfire. Billy Pine swung his shotgun up, but was drilled through the head by Holman before he could fire. Although the driver fired at the two businessmen, he took a bullet in the heart from Henry Smith, but then they both went down in a hail of hot lead from the gunrunners. When the smoke cleared, Holman and his men were unscathed, but Pine, Benson, Quayle, and Smith were dead.

Becky Sue and Patty Moore had sat inside the

stagecoach screaming all the while the guns were blazing outside. Their nightmare worsened when, weeping in terror, the two young women were forced outside and made to climb into the wagon. After the remaining crate of rifles was unloaded, the bodies of the four men were tossed inside the coach, and then the stagecoach was driven to the bank of the North Platte River. After the team was unhitched and set free, the coach was pushed into the water.

Taken along as hostages, Becky Sue and Patty were assured by Holman that they would be released unharmed once the exchange with the Indians had been made. The terrified sisters did not believe the rough-looking man, but they were helpless to do anything but await their fate.

Chapter Eight

The purple twilight was fading into darkness as Captain Vint Lonegan and Lieutenant William Louis Beaumont bellied down on the grassy crest of a knoll less than two hundred yards from the Hotamitanui encampment. The huge fire in the center of the compound threw flames high into the air, and dozens of drums echoed across the rolling hills as the fire dance began.

Lonegan had laid out the plan carefully to his friend. When he had sneaked to the camp the night before to see Little Star, he had found six sentries posted at various spots. They would each eliminate three sentries by knocking them out and tying them to trees, using—in what the captain thought a nice piece of irony—the same rope used to hang Lonegan over the stakes. Once the men were knocked out, they would gag the sentries with their own loincloths so they could not call out an alarm. There was no way to know how long the fire dance would last, but Lonegan and Beaumont had to be ready in plenty of time, and the wait could be long. They would do their best not to harm any of the guards, for Lonegan hoped that once Three Hands had been exposed as a murderous traitor and this ordeal was over, he might establish a relationship with Burning Sun. That purpose would be better served if in

112

taking Little Star from the camp, he left no dead sentries.

With that part of the plan taken care of, Lonegan and Beaumont would make their way to the rope corral and bridle pintos for Little Star and the deserters to ride. They would then lead the four animals to the spot where Lonegan and Beaumont's own horses were stashed a short distance down the Blue River. The bound subchief would ride on Beaumont's horse with him to ensure that he would not get away.

Looking at each other and nodding their readiness, the officers bent low and moved toward the camp. Cheyenne drums continued to beat out the rhythm for the fire dance as the two men crept along the bank of the river and peered through the trees. Several dozen Dog Men in full feathered regalia danced in a circle around the fire, the bells on their ankles giving off a synchronized jingling sound, while hundreds of celebrants in the outer circle blended their voices in a ritualistic chant.

Seated on the ground near the fire was the medicine man, who was painted extravagantly and wore the skin of a wolf. The hollowed-out wolf's head hung over his brow, with the rest of the hide covering his back. Periodically he tossed a pinch of gunpowder into the flames, sending up a flash followed by a blue-white puff of smoke.

Neither Burning Sun nor Three Hands was in sight, but Lonegan and Beaumont could see the three deserters, who were still tied to the trees. Their faces were drawn and haggard, and the copper paint on their near-naked bodies now revealed streaks of white skin.

Both men were glad for the loud noises that filled the camp. The shrill chant of hundreds of voices, the jingling bells on the ankles of the dancers, the thunder of the drums, and the roar of the fire would drown out any sounds made while putting the sentries out of commission and getting the horses out of the rope corral. It also helped that the corral was some distance from the last row of tepees. It caught little light from the big fire in the center of the compound.

Glancing up at the sky, Lonegan saw streaks of light peeking through the breaks in the clouds from the rising moon. He turned to the Frenchman and said, "Time to put a few sentries to sleep. Meet you shortly at the corral."

"It's a date," Beaumont responded with a grin.

It took the better part of half an hour for Vint Lonegan and William Louis Beaumont to accomplish their task. All six sentries had been overcome, bound, gagged, and tied to trees. The four pintos were led downriver, and then the men returned to their original base among the trees near the river and looked again toward the roaring fire.

Three Hands was now standing near it. Clad in beaded buckskin shirt and leggings and wearing his full headdress, the subchief watched the ceremonial dancing and singing with obvious enjoyment, clearly anticipating the moment when Little Star would be his. Gazing at his enemy, the captain muttered a foul oath under his breath.

On the opposite side of the fire, near the path that led to his big tepee, was Burning Sun. Standing unmoving despite the commotion going on around him, his face was an inscrutable mask.

"Looks like everybody's in place," whispered Lonegan. "Maybe it won't be too long now."

"Good," breathed Beaumont. "I'd like to get this thing over with." After a pause, he added, "I just had an ugly thought."

"What's that?"

"Maybe Little Star doesn't love you enough to buck her daddy's authority. I mean, maybe she won't run away with you."

"I have no question what she'll do, my friend,"

replied Lonegan, "but just the same I'll offer her a choice."

"Well, I sure hope for your sake she'll—"

The lieutenant cut short his words at the sudden, total silence when the drums, the chants, and the dancing all stopped at the same split second. Then Burning Sun raised his hands high. Lonegan urgently whispered, "You better get over there behind Three Hands and be ready. Remember . . . you make the first move."

"It'll be my pleasure!" replied the Southerner, and then he was gone.

Abruptly, the drums began to rumble again, but this time at a lower volume and with a different beat. Above them, the groom raised his voice in a Cheyenne love call to the bride. When the song was finished, the drums stopped again. A long, tense moment followed as Burning Sun walked to his tepee. He opened the flap and then stepped back, and the drums began to rumble again. Everyone in the camp looked toward the chief's tepee in complete silence. Not even a child made a sound. Three Hands stood completely still, except for the feathers in his headdress dancing in the breeze.

Vint Lonegan felt his heart hammer against his ribs as Little Star appeared in her doeskin dress. She was the most beautiful woman he had ever seen. Little Star took her father's arm, and her face was like granite—although there was obvious sorrow in her large dark eyes. She seemed to be purposely avoiding her father's gaze, and lifting her chin resolutely, she squared her shoulders and looked straight ahead.

The chief and his daughter started the slow walk toward the spot by the fire where Three Hands stood with a look of conquest on his cruel face. With every eye riveted on them, no one heard the soft footfalls from the edge of the darkness as William Louis Beaumont moved in like a swift-footed deer.

Burning Sun and Little Star were about thirty feet from the groom when suddenly the headdress was snatched from Three Hands's head and his neck was locked in the crook of Beaumont's arm. In the same smooth move, the Colt .45 muzzle was jammed just below his right ear, and the ominous sound of the hammer's being thumbed back filled the silent camp.

Holding the surprised subchief in an iron grip, the lieutenant shouted, "Nobody move!"

Burning Sun froze in his tracks, and hundreds of Hotamitanui faces registered shock. Little Star looked puzzled, obviously trying to determine what was happening.

Gazing at the aging chief, the Southerner bellowed, "Burning Sun! There's a hair trigger on my gun! No bullet, knife, or arrow could keep it from firing if I was hit! You better tell your people that!"

Quickly, the chief made the situation clear to his people in their own language. Although obviously chafing at the command, every Dog Man stayed where he was. Sweat appeared on the subchief's face, but he made no move to break himself free.

Setting his wary eyes on Beaumont, Burning Sun asked, "What is it you want, white man?"

Even as the chief was asking the question, a broad-shouldered form materialized out of the deep shadows behind the three prisoners. Little Star saw Vint Lonegan, and her eyes widened in disbelief. The muscular captain moved into Three Hands's view and saw the shock hit him. Glaring at him, Lonegan grunted, "We meet again!"

The subchief's dark face went black with rage, but still he made no move or sound.

Little Star waited beside her father, relief and happiness evident on her beautiful face.

Remaining where he stood, Lonegan said firmly, "Chief Burning Sun, we are taking your three prisoners with us. They will face the Army's court for what they have done. Colonel Harrington will know the truth about the raids, and I am sure an apology will be forth-coming to you from him."

The old chief reluctantly nodded. "You are taking only the prisoners?"

Little Star flicked a glance at her father and then looked back at Lonegan, who explained evenly, "I have also come to take Little Star with me—that is, if she wishes to go. I intend to make her my squaw if she does."

Burning Sun turned and looked at his daughter, his face devoid of expression. The beautiful maiden pulled her gaze from Vint Lonegan and looked her father in the eye, her decision obvious. He read her expression and then grunted, "Little Star will no longer be my daughter."

She flinched, and although the words had obviously cut deep, Little Star responded calmly, "It is not my desire for you to disown me, my father, for I love you very much. But having to be the squaw of a man I despise would be nothing but a living death. I am very much in love with Captain Vint Lonegan, and although I sorrow in your disowning me, I will be most happy as the squaw of the man I love."

Little Star kissed her father's weathered cheek and turned, briefly facing the subchief. Three Hands burned her with his blazing eyes, but she met his gaze with a proud look on her face. She then walked over to the big white man who had captured her heart.

Lonegan moved quickly, cutting the prisoners loose but leaving their hands tied in front of them. He then told Burning Sun, "We are taking Three Hands with us. If no one follows, we will set him free un-harmed when we are a safe distance away. However, if we are followed by even one warrior, I will personally kill him. Do you understand?"

"I understand," the old man answered with a nod, clearly wishing for the safety of his favorite warrior. "You will not be followed. I give you my word."

With that, Lonegan stepped to the subchief and bound his hands behind him. Signaling to the others, they hurried from the encampment and minutes later, six horses thundered along the bank of the Blue River, heading south. Beaumont was out in front, riding double with Three Hands, followed by Little Star and Lonegan, who held the lead ropes of the deserters' horses behind him.

The Southerner rode pressing the muzzle of his .45 revolver against the base of the subchief's skull. Above the rumble of galloping hooves, Three Hands shouted over his shoulder, "I will track you down, white-eyes pig, and slit your throat from ear to ear!"

Beaumont turned his head and shouted over his shoulder, "Vint! Did you hear what this traitor just said?"

"I heard it!" responded Lonegan.

"How about if I do the world a favor and blow his head off?"

"Only if we see someone on our trail!" called the captain. "We have to keep our promise to Burning Sun!"

Gritting his teeth, Beaumont pushed the muzzle of his revolver harder against the base of Three Hands's skull and hissed loudly, "I sure do wish some Dog Men would follow!"

The wide North Platte River finally came into view, gleaming in the moonlight. The waters churned where the Blue emptied into the North Platte, and Lonegan hollered for Beaumont to haul up as they neared the confluence. The horses snorted and blew as Lonegan and Beaumont dismounted, with both men holding fast to the animals' reins. Gazing behind them, the captain studied the moonlit prairie for a long moment.

When Lonegan turned back, Beaumont asked, "No one following?"

"Nope. I didn't think there would be. Burning Sun

is all too fond of this snake—although for the life of me, I can't figure out why." Moving toward the Southerner's mount, Lonegan said, "Let's get him down."

Three Hands was taken off the horse, and Lonegan removed the rope that held his wrists behind his back. "Okay, you can start walking," he said evenly. "If you don't dawdle, you'll be back to the camp before dawn."

Rubbing his wrists, the muscular Cheyenne eyed Lonegan and Beaumont with loathing and rasped, "I will find you and kill you! As slowly and as painfully as possible!"

"You'll be better off to forget us," Lonegan retorted. "Burning Sun is not going to sanction you giving chase as long as Little Star is with us. He may say he's disowned her, but she's still his flesh and blood. He won't want her put in any danger."

The subchief glared at the captain and then turned and pointed a stiff finger at the beautiful maiden. "I will come after you, Little Star!" he warned. "You will still become my squaw!"

The black-eyed beauty's face darkened. Fixing him with a steely stare, she spat, "I will not become your squaw! I am going to marry the man I love!"

Breathing heavily with rage, Three Hands growled, "If you will not marry me, you will not live to marry Vint Lonegan! I will kill you!"

Fury boiled up in Lonegan. He stormed at the muscular Indian, and before Three Hands could evade him, the big captain lashed out with a ferocious punch, knocking the Indian down. Standing over the dazed man, Lonegan cautioned, "You'd better never even try to get near Little Star, you snake-bellied traitor! It would be a pleasure to kill you with my bare hands, and that would give me an excuse to do it!"

With that, Lonegan strode to his horse, telling his lieutenant, "We need to cross the river and head toward the hideout. I want to be almost there when we stop for the night."

"Why not attack the hideout as soon as we get there?" Beaumont asked.

Lonegan shook his head. "Too risky. We have no idea of their setup—how many sentries, if any; the lay of the land . . . not to mention we'll be exhausted from pushing ourselves so hard. No, it's best to get a few hours' sleep, then hit them in the morning."

The captain was about to mount up when Three Hands leapt to his feet to attack him. Before he could reach him, however, William Louis Beaumont whipped out his right-hand gun and cracked the Indian over the head with it. The subchief's legs crumpled, and he fell to the ground unconscious.

Lonegan pivoted and looked down at his enemy and then at Beaumont. Holstering the gun, the lieutenant explained, "He was coming after you."

Lonegan knelt beside Three Hands. "He'll be out awhile," Lonegan declared after a moment. Rising, he mounted up and looked back at Todd Dressler and asked, "Which way is the hideout? I intend to get there in time to stop Clete Holman before the repeater rifles get into the hands of the Dog Men."

A sneer curled Dressler's upper lip. "How come you rode south out of the camp if you don't know where the hideout is?"

"I heard Three Hands say the rifles were to be kept on a small island in the middle of the North Platte. I figure the hideout can't be too far from the river, then. That's why. Now, which way is it?"

The corporal's chin jutted stubbornly. "I'm not telling you—and my men won't, either."

"Look," sighed the captain, "you've got some pretty stiff charges to face. Now, you lead me to the hideout, and I'll see that Colonel Harrington knows you cooperated."

"Our helping you won't cut no ice with Harrington," countered Dressler. "We're not ratting on our pals."

Lonegan shrugged his wide shoulders and said, "Okay, have it your way. Lieutenant Beaumont, let's remove their moccasins, then take them off their horses and retie their hands behind their backs."

"Wait a minute!" shouted Alf Kyle. "What're you doin'?"

Grinning crookedly, Lonegan replied, "We're taking the pintos and leaving you in your bare feet. I've got a feeling some Dog Men may come looking for Three Hands if he doesn't show up at the camp by sunrise. Some of them may not be in league with Three Hands—and they'll want to rush you back to the camp to face their very angry chief. But you can run barefooted and with your hands tied behind you, can't you? You'll have to, 'cause if they catch you and take you back to Burning Sun, you'll be in a heap of trouble."

The prisoners all seemed to deflate. Todd Dressler licked his lips nervously and asked, "You really think the colonel might go easier on us if we lead you to the hideout?"

"Could mean the difference between execution and prison."

"Okay," agreed Dressler, swallowing hard. "We'll do it."

Lonegan smiled and faced forward. He was about to spur his mount when Little Star suddenly declared, "Vint, please explain something to me. You called Three Hands a traitor. I, too, have the deepest loathing for him, but what is your reason for calling him that? And what is this about repeater rifles getting into the hands of the Dog Men?"

"It'll take a little while to tell you everything, honey," Lonegan replied. "I'll tell you about it when we stop. Right now, we need to get going."

As they rode south, Lonegan was wishing he had been able to keep Little Star in some safe place while he and Beaumont undertook the task of halting the delivery of the rifles to Three Hands and his men. But there was nowhere to take her. It troubled him, knowing that when he answered her questions, he was going to have to tell her about the subchief's plot to kill her father. Though there was no danger of its happening until Three Hands had the rifles, still the news would be very upsetting to Little Star.

They continued on at a steady trot when suddenly Todd Dressler pointed out a grove of trees up ahead, saying they should rest there for the night. The hideout was only about a mile and a half away.

The prisoners were allowed to dismount. Their hands were then tied behind their backs, and they sat on the ground, leaning against trees.

Little Star abruptly stepped in front of Lonegan and demanded, "Vint, you will tell me now about Three Hands being a traitor."

Towering over the small maiden, the captain complied, explaining how Three Hands went against her father's orders and had tried to kill him on the stakes. He also told her how the subchief had been stirring up trouble with the army by supplying Todd Dressler and his men with Cheyenne horses, clothing, and weapons for their raids. As Little Star listened intently, Lonegan recounted how Three Hands planned to get repeater rifles from Clete Holman and use them to lead the Hotamitanui Cheyenne into war with the whites.

Little Star's eyes narrowed in anger. "My father does not want war with the whites! Is Three Hands so foolish as to think his small group of followers can stir all the rest of the Dog Men to go to war against my father's wishes? When Burning Sun learns of this, he will have Three Hands and his followers tortured to death! They are indeed traitors!"

Lonegan cleared his throat and said, "Little Star, Three Hands does not intend to face Burning Sun's wrath. He has plans to murder your father once the rifles are in his hands."

The maiden was stunned. "This cannot be!" she gasped.

"I'm afraid it is. I heard Three Hands say so when I was hanging above the stakes. He figures to make it look like white men murdered Burning Sun, and since he would no doubt be made chief upon your father's death, he would then arm all the Dog Men and incite them to avenge Burning Sun's murder on all the whites."

Little Star asked, "Vint, I do not understand. Why did you not tell my father of Three Hands's vile scheme when you were in the camp earlier?"

"It would have been my word against his sub-chief's. Which one of us do you think he would believe?"

Little Star sighed. "Yes, you are right. But tell me, why did you let Three Hands go free to return to the camp? We must go back immediately and warn my father!"

"It would still be only my word against his," responded Lonegan. "If I had kept Three Hands our prisoner so he couldn't return to the camp, your father would have thought that I had gone against my word. He would've sent a horde of Dog Men after us, and we'd be in terrible trouble. The best thing for us to do is to stop the rifles from being delivered."

"But he may decide to go ahead and murder my father!" she protested.

"No, he won't, honey," Lonegan assured her in a soothing voice. "He has to make it look like white men did it so as to make the Dog Men ready to fight—but he definitely doesn't want to go to war without the repeater rifles. Your father is in no danger until Three Hands has the weapons, and we've got to keep that from happening. Once the delivery of the repeaters has been thwarted, we'll find a way to expose Three Hands for the foul traitor that he is. It could be that if we give him enough rope, he'll hang himself."

Todd Dressler suddenly interrupted, "Captain, if

everybody's at the hideout when we attack, there'll be eleven men. How are you and the lieutenant gonna take on that many?"

"We'll work it out," Lonegan replied drily.

"Look, maybe it'd favor us at the court-martial if the three of us help you against the gang and get the rifles," Dressler declared helpfully. "You and the lieutenant both've got rifles in your saddle boots, and the lieutenant wears two guns. Arm each of us and the odds'll be a whole lot better.

Lonegan gave the corporal a wry grin. "Nice try, Dressler, but forget it. Somehow I get the feeling you might just shoot Beau and me in the back and take off."

The ex-corporal started to protest his innocence of such thoughts, but then he apparently realized it was fruitless and became silent.

Little Star spoke up and said, "Vint, I am a crack shot with a rifle. Let me help you."

Looking at her tenderly, the big man put his hands on her shoulders and responded, "I appreciate your offer, but I can't allow you to be endangered. You'll remain a safe distance from the hideout and keep guard over these three while Beau and I find a way to capture the gang."

Then he took her by the hand and led her a short distance away from the others. Looking into her eyes, he whispered, "I think it's high time we give each other a proper greeting, don't you?"

Smiling up at him, Little Star replied, "I do."

Lonegan chuckled. "Remember those two words. You'll be using them very shortly, if I have my way."

She looked at him quizzically, but before she could say anything, he bent down and kissed her. Their arms locked around each other, and their kiss was both passionate and loving. Finally, breathless, they turned and walked back to the others. They would need all the rest they could get before tomorrow's battle.

Chapter Nine

Reaching the Hotamitanui encampment shortly after sunrise, Three Hands found Chief Burning Sun and his people gathered together, watching as the subchief and the other riders slowly made their way to the center of the compound. Three Hands rode his own pinto and was flanked by several braves whom Burning Sun had sent after his favorite warrior at the crack of dawn, certain that Vint Lonegan would keep his word and release him when they were a safe distance away.

The chief stepped close as Three Hands slid from his horse and, eyeing the lump on the subchief's head, asked, "Why were you hit?"

"Vint Lonegan gave me no reason," lied the traitor. "He brutally hit me with his revolver, knocking me unconscious. When I woke up, they were gone."

"You must sit down and rest," said the old chieftain. "I will have some food brought to you."

"There is no time to rest," Three Hands countered quickly. "I will take my warriors and pursue them. Vint Lonegan and the white-eyes pig who helped capture me will die, and I will bring the Cheyenne impersonators back to receive our justice! Your daughter will be returned to you also." He paused a few seconds and then added, "That is, unless my chief really meant she is no longer his daughter."

Inward pain showed in the eyes of the aging chief. "She is still my daughter," he murmured softly. "And for that reason I am not sure Three Hands should go after them. It could place Little Star in grave danger. Vint Lonegan will not give her up without a fight. She could be seriously hurt—or even killed."

Shaking his head, the subchief argued, "Vint Lonegan will surrender before he will endanger Little Star, my chief. And I need not assure you that Three Hands will do nothing to place her in jeopardy." The traitor laughed to himself, for what he did not tell the Cheyenne chief was that he had every intention of hurting her. In fact, he planned to kill her for shaming him in front of his people by choosing the white man over him.

Burning Sun seemed so shattered by the recent events that he almost appeared to have lost the will to live. Shaking his head, he declared softly, "I do not know if this should be done. Little Star's rebellion against her people has caused me great grief. Perhaps she should be allowed to live among the forebears of her mother's people." He sighed deeply and then added, "But you have always shown wisdom, Three Hands. Therefore, you have my blessing."

He then glanced toward Hungry Wolf, who was just under the subchief in the command chain, and told Three Hands, "You will take Hungry Wolf with you, for I have great confidence in him. He has always been most fond of Little Star and has been like a brother to her. The two of you will bring my daughter back safely."

The aging chief then gave orders not to be disturbed until Three Hands returned with his daughter. With that, he turned and walked somberly back to his tepee to go into seclusion.

Three Hands watched him go, his mind unsettled by the order to include Hungry Wolf in the search party. His presence would complicate things, for he was totally loyal to the chief—but the subchief had to do as Burning Sun had commanded, otherwise suspicion would be raised.

As the traitor led his nearly forty men in a hard gallop due south, he was formulating a story to explain the absence of the three braves who had accompanied him when Vint Lonegan had been taken from the camp. The subchief was sure they were dead—and that Lonegan's friend was responsible. Suddenly his head started throbbing, and he touched the spot where the man called Beaumont had clouted him. Seething with anger, Three Hands thought what a pleasure it would be to cut off the hand that had clouted him . . . before the man died.

He dug his heels into his pinto's sides, anxious to catch his enemies. He was sure Vint Lonegan would go to the hideout in an attempt to stop delivery of the rifles, and it was there that he was leading his warriors. If Lonegan had been to the hideout and gone, the subchief would then head for the island in the North Platte River. One place or the other, Three Hands would catch up to Lonegan and his companions—and then the two white men and the woman who had spurned him would die.

Observing Hungry Wolf from the corner of his eye, the subchief wondered what the warrior would do when he learned of Three Hands's plan to kill the chief and his daughter. Although Hungry Wolf wanted his people to regain their ancestral lands, he might well refuse to kill Burning Sun as part of the plan. Three Hands realized he would probably have to kill Hungry Wolf first, for he was bent on two things: He was going to become chief of the Dog Men band, and he was going to lead them into all-out war against the white men who had invaded their sacred land. No one was going to stand in his way.

* * *

After waking soon after sunrise the following morning some two hundred yards from the hideout, Captain Vint Lonegan led his group into a cluster of trees. The three deserters were tied to trees and gagged; then Lonegan pulled his Winchester .44 seven-shot repeater rifle from the saddle boot and handed it to Little Star.

"Keep an eye on our friends, here," he told her sternly. "Beau and I will be back as soon as possible."

"Have you figured out how you are going to capture so many men?" asked the beautiful young maiden.

Stroking his mustache thoughtfully, Lonegan replied, "Can't do that until we see the place. Once we're in close and get a look at the situation, we'll know what to do."

The two officers then took leather sheaths holding long-bladed knives from their saddlebags and strapped them on their belts. Beaumont took his own repeater rifle from its boot and suggested, "Vint, why don't you take this? I've got my two revolvers."

Lonegan nodded. "Good idea." He then took out extra cartridges for the rifle from his saddlebag. Turning to Beaumont, he said, "Okay, let's get this done."

Little Star stepped up to the big captain and hugged him tightly. Releasing him, she remarked, "Vint, I do not like to see only two of you going against so many. I am a very good shot with a rifle. I wish you—"

"No, honey," cut in Lonegan, shaking his head. "You'll be much safer here. We'll be back. I promise."

He squeezed her shoulder reassuringly, and then the officers crouched low and hurried toward the hideout that was nestled among a thick stand of trees. They covered the last fifty yards on their knees and elbows, staying hidden in the tall grass.

The Yankee and the Rebel crawled in close, facing the side of the house. Through the window they could see the men inside eating breakfast and laughing heartily.

Looking around, Lonegan saw no sign of any of the deserters outside. He turned to his lieutenant and whispered, "It couldn't be better. They're all in one spot. We'll work our way to the back, then bolt through the door and get the drop on them. I'll go in first."

"Yes, sir!" snapped Beaumont.

"Now, remember," breathed the captain, "we want them alive if possible. But if they go for their guns, shoot to kill. We won't get a second chance."

Pulling out his revolvers, the southerner thumbed back the hammers, and Lonegan quietly levered a cartridge into the chamber of the rifle. "Okay," he whispered, "let's move."

But just as both men raised up on their knees, a man came out the back door, and they quickly ducked. The man stepped off the porch and hurried across the yard to the privy that was in the trees some seventy feet from the house.

As soon as he had gone inside, closing the door behind him, Lonegan breathed, "We'll get him when he comes out and find out how many more are in the house."

As the officers crept up beside the outhouse, a burst of laughter came from the open kitchen door. Several minutes passed. Loud talking and intermittent gusts of laughter continued to come from the kitchen. Lonegan and Beaumont eyed each other with exasperation. How much longer would the man stay in the privy?

Then the waiting was over. The deserter stepped out into the brilliant sunlight, buckling his belt, when suddenly Lonegan had him in his iron grasp with a hand clamped over his mouth. The man's eyes bulged with fear when Beaumont's knife was placed against his throat.

"Don't struggle or you're a dead man!" warned the Southerner.

They dragged the man into the deep shade of the surrounding trees, and while the lieutenant kept the knife at the man's throat, Lonegan said threateningly, "I want some information, mister, so I'll have to let go of your mouth. But my partner's a cutthroat from way back, and if you even look like you're going to cry out, that blade will be buried in your throat. Got it?"

Sweating profusely, the man nodded emphatically. His eyes were fixed on Beaumont's hand, and his neck strained to avoid the tip of the blade.

The captain pulled his hand away from the frightened man's mouth and said, "Are you one of the deserters or one of Holman's men?"

The man's eyes bulged even larger, and he was obviously surprised at Lonegan's knowledge. Swallowing with difficulty, he choked, "I'm, uh, one of the deserters."

"What's your name?"

"Casper Snead," he responded hoarsely.

"How many men inside the house?"

"Six."

"All Dressler's men?"

Clearly puzzled about how Lonegan knew so much, Snead replied, "Yes, sir."

"Where are Clete Holman and his men?"

For an instant, it appeared as though Snead was going to balk. Beaumont pressed the sharp tip of the knife till it nicked the skin, and a tiny bubble of blood appeared. Jerking from the pain, the deserter answered, "They're probably on their way here right now."

"From where?"

"An island in the North Platte River about ten miles upstream. That's where they've got the rifles."

"All six hundred of them?"

"I'm . . . I'm not sure. Clete was expecting the last shipment of 'em to arrive on a stagecoach at Oshkosh late yesterday afternoon. If they got there as expected, he and his boys will be coming here."

"To close the deal with Three Hands, right?"

Snead swallowed hard again. "H-how do you know so much?"

"Answer the man's question!" the Frenchman ordered, pricking him with the knife again.

"I don't know, exactly!" the man fearfully whispered. "One of the Dog Men was supposed to be here so when the rifles were all on the island, he could ride and inform Three Hands we were ready to close the deal. The rifles came in a few days earlier than we expected, so our timing's off a bit. All I know is Clete and his boys are supposed to come here once all the rifles are on the island."

"Plenty of ammunition, too, I'll bet," said Beaumont.

His eyes riveted on Beaumont's knife hand, the deserter licked his lips and said, "Yeah."

"So the Cheyenne can wipe out your white brothers."

Snead swallowed hard and then asked, "Who are you?"

"I'm Captain Vint Lonegan, U.S. Army, and this friendly gentleman is Lieutenant William Louis Beaumont. We are on special assignment to bring you deserters and the Holman bunch in. You're under arrest for desertion, murder, and gunrunning," Lonegan said sharply, "And you're going to face trial at Fort McPherson."

"Now, w-wait a minute, Captain!" gasped Snead. "You just said murder! You got me on desertion and gunrunning, okay. But I didn't murder anybody!"

"You're one of the bunch that's been masquerading as Cheyenne and pulling raids, aren't you?"

"Well, yeah, but I didn't kill anybody myself!"

"Don't give me that, Snead!" hissed the captain. "Plenty of people have been killed in those raids. You were in on it, therefore you're guilty of murder! We've already got Dressler, Kyle, and Nelms in custody. You're all going to face murder charges!"

The deserter sagged slightly. He had no more to say.

"What shall we do with him?" asked Beaumont.

The captain flicked a glance at the privy and said, "Let's tie him up in there."

Moments later, after binding and gagging the man with strips of cloth from his shirt, the two officers stepped back outside. Turning, they saw through the trees another of the deserters come out of the house. He was carrying a double-barreled twelve-gauge shotgun and calling Snead's name. Just as Lonegan reached for his rifle, the man spotted him and shouted angrily.

Suddenly Casper Snead set up a racket inside the outhouse, kicking the door savagely. The captain and his lieutenant ducked around the sides of the privy as the man on the porch raised the shotgun and fired both barrels, one behind the other. The double roar echoed among the trees, and the charges tore huge smoking holes in the privy. There was a high-pitched scream, and then the kicking stopped. When both Army officers peered around the privy again, the deserter was dashing into the house, yelling for the men to grab their guns.

"We'll have to fortify ourselves better than this," the captain directed quickly, looking around. "Too bad we couldn't have caught them all at the breakfast table." Then he saw an old hay wagon standing some forty feet away between the house and the barn. "Come on. Let's get to that hay wagon and flip it on its side. It's a whole lot wider than this privy."

Dashing toward the wagon, they were halfway there when guns began to bark from the windows of the house, and they immediately dove for cover behind a rust-covered water trough. Bellying down, they each took an end, popping shots at the windows and shattering glass. A shotgun boomed from the kitchen door, and the buckshot hit the trough, creating water spouts.

"Beau, old pal," breathed Lonegan, "I'd say we're pinned down here."

"What was your first clue?" the Frenchman retorted, unsuccessfully avoiding a stream of water. Then another round blasted the trough, and they both instinctively ducked.

Silence reigned from the house, and the officers decided the deserters were either planning their strategy or reloading—or both. Taking advantage of the lull, they raced to the old hay wagon and turned it on its side. The thick floorboards of the wagon bed were missing in several spots, giving them ideal slots from which to shoot.

Peering through the narrow slots, Beaumont whispered, "They're up to something. It's been quiet too long."

Taking advantage of the silence, Lonegan dutifully shouted loudly, "We're United States Government agents, and you men are under arrest! You'd be wise to surrender peacefully!"

The answer was two charges of buckshot ripping into the wagon bed, splintering the wood. Relieved that both of them were uninjured, Lonegan snapped, "That shotgunner has got to be eliminated. As far as I can determine, he shoots then pulls back on the right side of the door. If I can put a couple of shots through the clapboards in just the right spot, I think they'll pierce our friend."

So saying, the captain fired a .44 slug into the wall, then worked the lever and repeated the action. There was a scream and then suddenly the deserter staggered out the open doorway to the edge of the porch. The shotgun slipped from his fingers and clattered to the ground, and then he peeled off the porch and landed facedown beside his weapon. The captain's bullets had found their mark.

Beaumont abruptly yelled, "Crossfire!" and pointed at four men darting behind trees on the left and on the right. The lieutenant immediately sent a shot at one man who was swinging a gun around the tree where he had stopped. The slug hit him dead-center in the mouth, spraying blood as it came out the back of his head.

Lonegan fired at another of the deserters just as the man was leaning out to use his revolver. The slug tore bark and threw debris into his eyes, and he howled in pain while the others unleashed a barrage of shots at the men behind the overturned wagon.

A third man bolted from behind a cottonwood, taking refuge behind the privy and giving him a better angle from which to shoot. Vint Lonegan saw him sprint; then, guessing where the man would fire from, he lined his gunsight on the spot and waited. When the man's shoulder filled the sight, Lonegan fired. The slug tore through the man's right shoulder, and he grunted in pain, blood spurting, and drew back out of sight.

The man who had been momentarily blinded now was back in action, and he kept up a steady fire at William Louis Beaumont.

"I don't know know how much longer we can keep this up, Vint," Beaumont called above the racket. "We've been holding our own so far, but they've really got us pinned down. I don't—" His words were cut off when a bullet pinged into the iron banding around the wagon bed close to his head.

Then a man up on the roof fired, and Lonegan felt the bullet whiz terrifyingly close to his face. He peered around the wagon to see where the shot had come from and spotted the man, who was drawing a bead again.

Suddenly a rifle barked from behind a tree near the outhouse. The man on the roof stiffened, and the rifle fell from his hands and slid down the side of the roof. Arching his back, the deserter somersaulted off the roof and slammed onto the ground. There was a sudden break in the firing, and both Lonegan and Beaumont looked toward the source of the shot that had taken out the man on the roof. Little Star stood there, holding Vint Lonegan's smoking rifle.

Lonegan started to call to her when two of the deserters unleashed their guns again, one from each side. The captain and Beaumont were instantly occupied.

The wounded man behind the privy wheeled around when Little Star's rifle barked. Surprise filled the man's face as he stared at the young woman standing fifteen feet away from him. There was a moment's hesitation, then he slowly—and obviously painfully—brought his revolver up and took aim at her. But before he could fire, the maiden leveled the Winchester and pulled the trigger. Little Star's cartridge exploded his heart.

One of the two remaining deserters apparently realized that the tide had turned, and he sprinted from his cover toward the front of the house, trying to escape. He fired back at the overturned wagon as he ran, but William Louis Beaumont drew a bead and dropped him with one shot.

Vint Lonegan held his rifle ready, waiting for the last man to make his move. The old farmyard was suddenly as quiet as a cemetery. Then, breaking the silence, the man called out, "Bruce?"

No answer.

"Bruce!"

More silence.

Then Captain Vint Lonegan's wintry voice cut through the yard. "Give it up, fella, or you're a dead man!" Throw your gun out and put your hands behind your head; then come out real slow!"

The man stubbornly retorted, "I'm a dead man either way! I ain't lettin' you take me to the fort for a trial! Nobody's gonna put a rope around my neck!"

Even as he spoke, the desperate deserter came out around the tree, gun blazing. Lonegan and Beaumont put five bullets into his chest, split seconds apart, and the man's lifeless body flopped to the ground.

The thick silence returned. Slowly, cautiously, Little Star stepped out from behind the privy, rifle in hand, and the two men walked toward her. Lowering her head submissively, the Cheyenne maiden peered up at Lonegan and murmured, "I know you told me not to come, but I am glad I did."

A grin spread across the big man's face. "I am too," he confessed, taking her into his arms.

William Louis Beaumont looked at the bodies of Little Star's victims and then said admiringly, "That was some shooting! You can fight in my army anytime!"

"I agree," declared the captain. Then his face grew solemn, and he ordered, "We'd better get going. We need to capture that island before Three Hands claims the rifles."

The trio returned to where they had left Dressler and his men. After the deserters were untied from the trees but their hands left bound, the group mounted up, galloping hard toward the North Platte River.

Less than fifteen minutes later, Three Hands and his warriors rode up to the hideout and found the bloody carnage. Sidestepping Hungry Wolf's questions about who the dead men were and what was taking place, the subchief commanded his men on, and ramming their ponies' sides, they galloped in the direction of the island.

Chapter Ten

Lieutenant Carl Clendennan slowly led his six be-draggled, weary men southward toward the North Platte River. At sunrise, little more than an hour earlier, the patrol had been ambushed by a band of several dozen Oglala Sioux. A fierce battle had taken place, in which eighteen cavalrymen had been killed.

The fact that a number of Sioux had been killed or wounded was little comfort to Clendennan. Of the six survivors of his troop, two were badly wounded; Sergeant Harry Gilman still had a Sioux arrow in his left side, and Trooper Bob Davidson's left arm was gashed severely from a tomahawk. Looking back at the two men, he saw that they were losing blood rapidly, and Gilman was barely able to stay in the saddle as he rode doubled over.

Clendennan breathed a prayer of thanks that at least this many men had escaped death at the hands of the Sioux. Only because the Indians had spent all their arrows and run out of ammunition had they ridden away and allowed the seven soldiers to live.

Trying to encourage his men, the lieutenant told them, "We're only about a mile from the river. When we reach it, we'll rest for a while before beginning the ride east to Fort McPherson."

Soon the men in blue sighed with relief as the North Platte came into view. Pointing to a tree-covered island about a hundred feet long and fifty feet wide in the middle of the river, Clendennan said, "That's the ideal place to stop. We'll ford the river just downstream from that island, where the water should be a bit more shallow."

Ten minutes later the small column worked its way down the bank and into the river, and the water swirled up to their stirrups. Skirting the eastern side of the island, they moved slowly toward the southern tip and then began to traverse the seventy feet of river separating the island from the mainland.

Suddenly one of the men pointed in the direction from which they had just come and exclaimed, "Lieutenant! Look!"

Clendennan and his men reined in. Six riders were galloping furiously toward them, and four of the horses were pintos.

"What do you make of that, sir?" the trooper asked. "Looks like four Indians and two white men. No, wait a minute! One of those Indians is a woman!"

"They're being chased!" gasped Clendennan, rising in his stirrups and looking past the six oncoming riders. "Look!"

Visible across the sun-drenched prairie, a few miles behind the six riders, was a large band of Cheyenne warriors in hot pursuit.

Amid the trees and thick brush of the small island, Clete Holman stood talking with his three men, every once in a while glancing at his two hostages. Becky Sue and Patty Moore sat huddled on the ground nearby, their eyes averted from the men, clearly terrified that the outlaws would harm them before they let them go free.

Holman was in the middle of telling two of his men to contact Three Hands and tell him that the full shipment of rifles was on the island. But before he finished giving his orders, the gunrunner heard the rumble of galloping hooves from the mainland.

Making their way to the edge of the island, Holman and his men peered through the brush and saw six riders, pursued by the thundering band of Cheyenne, gallop out into the water. The gunrunner suddenly swore loudly. The riders were heading toward a group of battered cavalrymen, who were fording the river just downstream from the island.

"Look, boss!" one of the men gasped, pointing eastward. "Army!"

"I ain't blind!" the gunrunner growled. Signaling to his men, he quickly devised a plan.

Captain Vint Lonegan led his group into the river toward the men in blue. As they splashed toward the calvarymen, one of the troopers shouted, "It's Captain Lonegan, Lieutenant!"

Clendennan and Lonegan recognized each other immediately, and it was readily apparent to the captain that the soldiers had been in a fierce battle. He quickly explained that they were being pursued by Three Hands and his Dog Men warriors.

Wiping a weary hand across his mouth, Clendennan looked past Lonegan's group to the oncoming horde of yelping Cheyenne. "We're in trouble, Captain," he muttered glumly. "My men and I have just come through a brutal fight with some Oglalas. As you can see, two of them are in bad shape. We haven't got more than thirty rounds of ammunition between us."

As the pursuing Dog Men neared the river, Lonegan explained, "The reason Three Hands is coming this way is that there are six hundred new repeater rifles and plenty of ammunition waiting for him on that island. But undoubtedly a gunrunner named Clete Holman and three of his men are also there."

Hope showed in Clendennan's eyes. "Then there's only one thing to do," he said quickly. "Let's seek refuge on the island! We'll do what we have to with the gunrunners." Making haste, the riders lashed their horses farther into the water and headed for the island.

Clete Holman swore vehemently and yelped, "Those bluecoats are comin' here!"

"What're we gonna do, boss?" asked Harley Carter, his voice on the edge of panic. "If those Army guys see these rifles, we've had it!"

"We can't stop 'em now," responded Holman. "We'll just have to kill 'em after—" Suddenly Holman recognized the three near-naked men riding pintos. He gasped, "Look! That's Todd Dressler and two of his boys!" Looking back at the charging Dog Men, he added, "And that's gotta be Three Hands and his warriors!"

"Boss, if that's Three Hands comin', we'll be in good shape," spoke up Mickey Wilson. "We can just kill the soldiers and them other guys and carry on as planned."

"Yeah," snickered Holman. Then, focusing on Little Star, he grinned salaciously. "Yeah, that's what we'll do. And maybe I'll just keep that good-lookin' squaw for myself."

Minutes later, the men in blue and Lonegan's group forged onto the island and into the cover of the trees. They were about to dismount when suddenly Clete Holman's voice barked, "Hold it right there!"

The group looked toward the voice. The outlaw and his three men were holding guns on them.

"Hey, Clete!" shouted Todd Dressler. "It's me! Don't you recognize me?"

"Sure," Holman replied. From the side of his

mouth, he ordered, "Mickey, cut their ropes off so they can get down off them pintos."

Lester Nelms began to laugh and Alf Kyle shouted, "Whoopee! We're free!"

"Just a minute, Holman!" snapped Lonegan, eyeing him angrily. "I'm Captain Vint Lonegan, and you've committed enough crimes as it is. Freeing federal prisoners only makes your case worse!"

Holman sneered and retorted, "Do I look worried? Fact is, I don't much care who you are, 'cause I'm about to turn you over to Three Hands. And from the looks of the way he's after you, I'd say I'd be doin' him one mighty big favor." Gesturing with his revolver, he ordered, "Get down off your horses."

The soldiers and Lonegan's group silently obeyed.

Grinning, Holman commanded, "Mickey, Harley, collect everybody's guns while I keep 'em covered. Dick, go grab one of them new rifles and step out to the shoreline where Three Hands can see you. He no doubt saw these blue-bellies come on the island along with these people he's chasin', so he might be expectin' to get shot at. Show him the rifle and tell him we've got all six hundred. Tell him he can have Lonegan and his pals right now and go get the gold. When I see the gold, he'll get his rifles. Hurry up!"

Lonegan, Beaumont, and the soldiers were quickly disarmed while Dick Swope dashed to the stack of wooden crates nearby, pried one open, and removed a new Spencer repeater. Then he dashed through the thicket to the south shore of the island to wait for the Dog Men.

Suddenly into the clearing stepped the two young women. William Louis Beaumont immediately recognized the Moore sisters and, shocked, gasped, "What are you doing here?"

With a cry of joy, they dashed to him, and Becky Sue hurriedly told him their story.

Sneering, Clete Holman told them, "I'm afraid

your little reunion's gonna be cut short. Three Hands'll be here any minute."

Leaving his men fifty yards from the river, Three Hands trotted to the riverbank and sat on his pinto, gazing at the island and pondering the situation. Vint Lonegan and his group had met with a unit of soldiers in the middle of the river and then gone onto the island. He could not see through the thick brush, but he assumed there would be gunfire if Holman and his men were there. Wondering where Holman might be, he began figuring how to attack the island and wipe out the soldiers and Lonegan's group.

Just then Dick Swope stepped into view, carrying a rifle. Recognizing the man, the subchief narrowed his eyes suspiciously. The presence of Lonegan and the soldiers on the island with Clete Holman and his men with no fighting going on between them could only mean one thing: Holman was double-crossing him.

Furious, Three Hands was nonetheless not surprised. He had never completely trusted Holman anyway—he was a white man, after all. But what difference did it make? Had he not planned all along to kill Holman and his men, once he had the six hundred repeaters? This way, he had all of his white enemies trapped on the island, making it easier to kill them. He would also have the pleasure of killing the woman who had spurned him.

Glaring at Dick Swope, Three Hands levered a cartridge into the chamber of the nickel-plated repeater Holman had given him, while nudging his pinto to the edge of the riverbank. Dick Swope raised the new rifle in his hand and opened his mouth, but he never got to voice his words. Aiming at Swope's chest across seventy feet of water, Three Hands squeezed the trigger. The rifle bucked in his hands, and Swope was flung to his back by the impact of the slug.

Moments later a stunned Clete Holman broke

through the brush and shouted across the river, "Three Hands! What are you doin'?"

Shaking the rifle furiously, the subchief railed violently, "All on the island will die!" With that, he wheeled his horse around and galloped back to his waiting men.

Holman dashed back into the brush and said to his other two men, "Somethin's wrong! Those dirty redskins are gonna attack us! Break out them Spencers!"

"But boss," gasped Mickey Wilson, "what about the gold?"

"There ain't gonna be no gold!" spewed Holman. "Three Hands is double-crossin' us!"

Leaving his man open-mouthed, the outlaw leader ran to Lonegan and declared, "Look, Captain, we can settle our differences later, but we need each other now. I'm gonna give you and your men back your guns. You can use these Spencers, too. Okay?"

"Okay," nodded Lonegan, "but if we live through this—"

"Like I said," Holman interrupted, "that'll come later. None of us'll live through this unless we stick together."

Vint Lonegan looked across to the mainland. Three Hands and his warriors were massing at the shoreline with one thing in mind: massacre.

The rifles were quickly passed around to every able-bodied man on the island. Sergeant Harry Gilman could not fight, but Trooper Bob Davidson told his lieutenant he could fire from a prone position.

Becky Sue Moore said to the handsome Frenchman, "Mr. Beaumont, Patty and I have never fired a gun before, but if you show us how, we can load them for you."

Beaumont smiled at her. "Good. And I think under the circumstances, we can drop the formality. Call me Beau."

Becky Sue blushed, and her infatuation with the Southerner was evident—even with the danger in the air. She hung on his every word as he instructed them on how to load the repeaters.

Little Star joined the men at the open crates, picking up a Spencer and loading it. When Vint Lonegan went to his horse to get his own repeater, Clete Holman stepped up to Little Star and said with a lustful grin, "Can you handle one of these, little squaw?"

Fixing him with a hard glare, she responded while working the lever, "My name is Little Star. And yes, I can handle one of these."

Lonegan returned, stepping between them, and said, "Believe me, she can use it, Holman."

The outlaw leader took a step back and, looking at Little Star, asked, "You're Cheyenne, ain't you?"

"Yes," she replied tersely, testing the balance of the gun.

"How can you shoot your own kind?"

"They are traitors!" she snapped, anger flashing in her black eyes. "Three Hands is planning to murder my father and become chief of the Hotamitanui. His warriors follow him. I can shoot them with no difficulty!"

Three Hands stopped his warriors a few yards short of the river and said to Hungry Wolf, "Take a group of warriors and cross to the other side of the river. I will attack from this side."

Worry was evident in Hungry Wolf's dark eyes. "Is Three Hands forgetting that Little Star is on the island?" he asked pointedly. "If we attack, one of our bullets could find her."

Three Hands sniffed angrily. "Vint Lonegan will see that she is protected. Hurry! We must attack!"

Reluctantly, Hungry Wolf led his group of men across to the far shore at a spot farther downstream and then moved the column back toward the island.

* * *

Seeing the move by the Dog Men, Vint Lonegan told Clete Holman, "We'd better split up just like they have. We're going to get it from both sides."

Nodding, Holman took his two men and the three deserters to the north side of the island, while the big captain stayed on the south side, keeping the woman he loved with him.

Suddenly there was a wild cry as Three Hands raised his rifle and led his twenty men in a charge toward the river. As the horses hit the water, Cheyenne guns began roaring from both sides of the river, and those on the island opened fire in return.

For almost half an hour guns blazed. Several of Three Hands's warriors fell under the gunfire, and their lifeless bodies floated down the river. The people on the island were crack shots, and they had superior weaponry and plenty of cover from the trees and brush, making it impossible for the Cheyenne and his men to make any gains. It would be much harder than Three Hands had thought to get the rifles. Abruptly he gave the signal for retreat and led his warriors onto the south bank and out of rifle range. Hungry Wolf pulled back on the north side and then rode down the bank until he and his men were at a safe distance from the island and crossed the river to join Three Hands.

When they were all massed, the subchief dismounted, telling the warriors to do the same. Then he said to Hungry Wolf, "It is clear that our enemies have the advantage. I think it would be better to throw a siege on them. They cannot have much food on the island. We can wait them out."

Hungry Wolf agreed. He reported that he had lost one man and did not want to lose any others.

Three Hands quickly sent several warriors to return to the encampment for food and additional ammunition, as well as bows and arrows. He then directed four braves to watch the island—two from where they stood and two from across the river on the far bank. They were to make sure no one left the island.

When the Indians pulled back, those on the island found that one trooper and one of Dressler's men had been killed. No one else had been hit, but Sergeant Harry Gilman had died from loss of blood. The bodies of the dead were placed out of sight at the west end of the island.

When they had gathered back together, Lieutenant Carl Clendennan looked at the assembled band and asked, "How long has it been since you people have eaten?"

Rubbing his empty stomach, Lonegan sighed and answered, "I think it's been about a month."

Clendennan directed a couple of his men to bring the remaining food in the army saddlebags, and Clete Holman then added whatever beans he had to the pot. The lieutenant handed out hardtack and beef jerky, saying the supply was low, but they would all share what was left.

Their hunger slightly mollified, Vint Lonegan looked around at the discouraged group and, trying to lift their spirits, remarked, "We shouldn't be stuck here too long. Certainly when the lieutenant's patrol doesn't return to Fort McPherson, Colonel Harrington will send out a search party."

Lieutenant Carl Clendennan sighed wistfully and said, "I wish you were right, Captain, but I'm afraid there'll be no search party. Some of our troops have been transferred to other forts of late, leaving McPherson without enough men to spare. And I fear that if Colonel Harrington gets word of the battle we fought this morning with the Ogallalas and we don't show up in a couple of days, he'll probably assume we were all killed. I hate to say it, but we may as well face reality. We'd best not plan on rescue coming from the fort."

One of the troopers looked at Lonegan and asked, "Captain, what do you think Three Hands is going to do?"

"Hard to say," replied the big man. "He may come at us again any time, or he may decide to be patient and starve us out. He has access to food. We don't. If he's got sentries posted on both sides of us, there's no way any of us can slip out and bring back food. Anybody who tried it would end up dead."

"Well, if he decides to lay a siege on us," said Clendennan, "we have one pretty good source of food —the horses."

Patty Moore flinched. Looking at the lieutenant with disbelief written all over her pretty face, she gasped, "You mean *eat* the horses?"

Clendennan smiled and replied, "I guarantee you, Miss Moore, horse meat will look pretty appetizing when you get hungry enough."

The group laughed—though the merriment was more forced than felt. The men then moved to the south shore of the island to see what the Cheyenne were doing on the prairie, leaving the women alone.

Introducing herself to the Moore sisters, Little Star learned that they had met William Louis Beaumont on the stagecoach from Scott City, Kansas, but after he had gotten off at McCook, Nebraska, he had disappeared. He had been nowhere to be found when it was time for the stage to leave, and they had not seen him again until he had landed on the island. It was obvious from the look in her eyes as she spoke of Beaumont that Becky Sue was quite taken with the dashing man from New Orleans.

Beaumont, meanwhile, was watching Clete Holman surreptitiously and thinking about Art Sands. Wanting to exact vengeance, he smiled grimly to himself. At least Three Hands had done one good thing: He had put a bullet through Dick Swope's wicked heart.

* * *

Night fell without another attack. A fire was built in the center of the island, and while the group was eating the last of the food, Clete Holman stared hungrily at Little Star. Catching him, she gave him a cold glare and then turned her attention to the handsome captain seated protectively beside her.

It was decided that the men would take turns keeping watch during the night, with one man on each side of the island at all times. The women would sleep close to the fire, and the men would sleep nearby.

Clete Holman took the first watch on the north side of the island, and Lieutenant William Louis Beaumont was on the south side. While the others were making preparations for sleep, Vint Lonegan took Little Star by the hand and led her into the brush until they were out of sight of the others. Folding her into his arms, he kissed her warmly. She clung to him, saying first that she loved him with all her heart and then expressing her fear that if Three Hands was not stopped soon, he would murder her father.

Holding her close, Lonegan said encouragingly, "Don't worry. We're going to survive this ordeal—and that dirty traitor will be stopped."

They kissed again and returned to the fire.

William Louis Beaumont was sitting near the river's edge with a rifle across his lap when he heard the rustle of leaves behind him. Turning sharply, he saw Becky Sue Moore come out of the brush. As she knelt down beside him and laid a hand on his arm, he told her sharply, "Young lady, you should be going to sleep."

"I will in a minute," she responded softly. "I just wanted to tell you that I'm glad you're on this island. I feel so much safer with you here."

The man from New Orleans had been around females enough to know that Becky Sue was infatuated with him. He decided that while he would not encourage the pretty young woman, neither would he dash her dreams, given their desperate circumstances —for there was more than a possibility that neither of them would get off the island alive. Patting the hand that rested on his arm, he told her sweetly, "I'm glad my presence makes you feel safer. Believe me, I'll do all I can to protect you."

"Thank you," she replied softly and then kissed his cheek. Rising to her feet, she whispered, "Good night."

"Good night," Beaumont echoed, smiling pleasantly. He watched her leave and then sighed. "I pray to God that it will be," he murmured.

Chapter Eleven

Dawn had barely broken when heavy rifle fire tore through the stillness. Splitting his ranks again, Three Hands had his warriors send a constant barrage from both sides of the river, keeping everyone on the island occupied. While the gun battle was raging, two braves sneaked onto the island from the west end and released all the horses, driving them into the river. The terrified animals swam downstream and then climbed to land, and soon they were in the hands of the Dog Men. The flying bullets wounded three warriors, but no one was killed, and having accomplished their purpose, the Cheyenne once again pulled back out of rifle range.

Seeing the animals flee, the occupants of the island realized that Three Hands had thought as they had: The horses would have given them plenty of food to withstand a siege—and it was now evident that that was what the subchief had in mind. With their food source gone, the islanders found it hard not to despair, and they waited anxiously to see what would happen next.

When darkness fell, Three Hands prepared his men to launch their next assault. Sitting beside their campfire, he explained that they would again attack from both sides of the river, only this time they would send hundreds of arrows over the trees to fall onto the island. Many of the arrows would be deflected by trees and brush—but some would surely find white flesh.

Suddenly Hungry Wolf leapt to his feet and glared down at Three Hands. He sternly argued, "Have you forgotten that our arrows can also find *red* flesh? Little Star is on that island—or have you forgotten that also!"

Three Hands stood up as well and angrily retorted, "Little Star has made her choice: to be with the white man named Lonegan. I am no longer concerned with her safety—I am concerned about getting those six hundred rifles! With those weapons, the Hotamitanui will rid Cheyenne land of white-eyes invaders!"

Narrowing his eyes, Hungry Wolf demanded, "You would sacrifice our chief's daughter for rifles?"

"Not for rifles," railed Three Hands. "For our nation!"

Hungry Wolf's face was filled with anger. "No one can be loyal to the mighty chief Burning Sun and take the life of his daughter!"

Sniffing derisively, Three Hands regarded the warrior coolly. "Your mighty chief is a white-bellied coward who would negotiate with white eyes! He deserves no loyalty! I will kill Burning Sun, and then this deserving warrior will become chief of the Hotamitanui! I will lead our people into battle, and we will kill all white eyes!"

"So it is *you* who are the traitor!" Hungry Wolf roared. Going berserk with wrath, the warrior screamed like a banshee and lunged at Three Hands, seizing his throat. But several braves immediately grabbed him, roughly yanking him away from their leader and holding him in check.

Breathing heavily, the malevolent subchief calmly picked up his nickel-plated rifle and pointed it at Hungry Wolf. His eyes filled with evil, he looked at the man who had attacked him and hissed, "You die!" To the braves who held him, he growled, "Let go of him."

When Hungry Wolf stood alone, facing the ominous muzzle, Three Hands declared, "I will give Hungry Wolf a chance. Run!"

"No!" countered the warrior, shaking his head. "If you are going to kill me, do it looking me in the eye. I will not run!"

Sneering, the traitor said coldly, "As you wish," and squeezed the trigger.

The rifle barked, sending its echo across the moon-lit prairie, and Hungry Wolf hit the ground. Carrying his smoking rifle, the killer stood over the still form, staring at his former friend for a moment. Then, looking at a couple of his braves, he commanded, "Throw him in the river."

The two braves obeyed, dragging Hungry Wolf's body to the river with Three Hands following. They tossed it in, and Three Hands stood on the riverbank, watching it float away.

The people trapped on the island were sitting around their campfire, eating the last of the food and discussing the incident they had seen a short while ear-lier. Hearing the rifle shot, they looked toward the moonlit shore and saw the body of a warrior being dragged to the river. It was apparent that one of the Dog Men had done something that displeased Three Hands, and he had paid for it with his life.

They all fell silent, lost in thought and staring into the flames of the fire. Then Little Star felt Clete Holman's lecherous eyes on her once again. Looking sharply at him, she gave him an icy glare, but he just smiled wickedly, wiping his mouth with the back of his hand.

The maiden turned to Vint Lonegan and sug-gested, "Let us take a walk."

He agreed, and they left the others, moving through the brush to the water's edge on the south side of the island. Suddenly the trooper keeping watch stood up, surprising the couple. Speaking softly, Lonegan asked, "Everything quiet, Price?"

"Yes, sir," reported the trooper. Then he cleared his throat slightly, and shyly offered, "If you want, I can move a bit farther down."

"No," the captain replied, grinning. "We'll do the moving. Keep your eyes peeled. Three Hands is a crafty one, and you never know what he might pull."

Walking to the end of the island, the couple stopped and gazed across the river to the prairie, which looked so peaceful bathed in the soft moonlight. They turned and faced each other and, as the moon passed behind a cloud bank, the captain folded Little Star in his strong arms. She removed his hat, running her fingers through his thick blond hair, and they enjoyed a long, lingering kiss. While the big man held her, the young woman considered telling him of the way Clete Holman had been looking at her, but she quickly decided against it. They did not need more trouble on the island than they already had. They kissed again, delighting in their time together, but then they finally—and reluctantly—decided they should return to the others.

As they passed near where Private Ben Price was hunkered at the shoreline, they heard a splash of water and stopped, listening intently and peering through the gloom. But the moon was behind the clouds again, and it was too dark to see anything.

Moments later, the sound was repeated just as the moon reappeared. They pushed their way through the brush toward the young soldier, whom they could see—though indistinctly—holding his rifle ready and searching the river.

Suddenly there was a rippling of water again. Price tensed, gripping his rifle. Then came a deadly hiss. A Cheyenne arrow struck Price in the throat, cutting off any sound. He fell backward into the bushes, rocking in agony and clutching at the arrow. He made a muffled, gagging sound and then died.

Horrified, Little Star and Lonegan raced back through the brush to warn the others.

Slightly beyond the campfire, Patty Moore was sitting on a fallen log beside Trooper Bob Davidson, and the two of them were talking quietly with each other about their lives and their families.

Davidson's words were suddenly obscured by a strange whispering noise. At first it sounded like a flock of birds winging low over the island, but then the "birds" began to strike. Cheyenne arrows, arched high over the trees, fell in a rain of death.

A feathered arrow whisked past Patty's ear, burying itself in Bob Davidson's chest. She started to scream, but it was cut off as an arrow tore into her head.

The people scattered. William Louis Beaumont immediately threw himself on top of Becky Sue Moore, shielding her body with his.

When the whirring sound ended, Harley Carter was moaning somewhere in the dark, calling to Clete Holman that he was hit in the leg. The others began to stir. Vint Lonegan had done as Beaumont had, protecting Little Star from harm by lying on top of her. Now he and the maiden hurried to the clearing by the fire, and the captain and the Southerner had started to confer when suddenly the whispering sound came again.

"More arrows!" shouted Lonegan, ducking his head as both he and Beaumont hovered over the women and dragged them deeper into the trees for better cover.

This time when the rain of arrows ceased, Lonegan called out, "Everybody stay under the trees! Don't go to the fire until we know this thing is over!"

He and Little Star cautiously sat up and looked around. Gazing across the clearing, the maiden suddenly saw the gruesome tableau of Bob Davidson with an arrow in his chest and Patty Moore lying partially across his body with an arrow through her head, its bloody tip protruding just in front of her left ear.

Fury surged through Little Star, and she felt as

though her veins were on fire. Holding her, Lonegan told her softly, "You're trembling. Don't be frightened."

"I am not frightened!" she exclaimed. "I am angry!"

Squirming loose from his hold, she dashed to where several loaded rifles leaned against a wooden crate, scooped one up, and bolted for the south edge of the island. Lonegan was on her heels, trying to stop her, but she dodged his hands. She levered a cartridge into the chamber, breaking through the brush so fast that she barely stopped at the water's edge. Looking across the river, the maiden saw several Dog Men exposed by the moonlight, retreating back to their camp.

Breathing fast, Chief Burning Sun's daughter shouldered the rifle, aimed carefully, and fired. One of the Indians threw his bow in the air, arched his back, and fell on his face. Little Star worked the lever, quickly taking aim again as the braves dived to the ground. Picking out the slowest one, she fired. The rifle bucked against her shoulder, and Three Hands lost another of his loyal warriors.

Whooping victoriously as she saw them fall, she herself then retreated back into the brush. Lonegan was waiting there and, laying a hand on her shoulder, scolded her mildly, saying, "You shouldn't have exposed yourself to such danger. One of them could have put an arrow through you."

Shaking her head, she countered, "What matters is that these traitors have paid for their treachery!"

Dawn came to the Nebraska plains, bringing the promise of a prolonged siege. Without food, all that the survivors on the island could do was drink river water to relieve their thirst—and they had to collect it at some risk.

Lieutenant Carl Clendennan made a mental count of the able-bodied. They were now down to eleven people who could handle a gun—that was, of course, if

Harley Carter could do so with his wounded leg. The officer was also worried about Alf Kyle, who was showing signs of breaking under the pressure.

Little Star took it upon herself to tend to Harley Carter's wound. After the attack the night before, she had removed the arrow from his leg, knowing how to extract it with the least amount of pain and damage.

A compassionate William Louis Beaumont tried to comfort Becky Sue Moore as she continued to grieve over the horrible death of her sister. While she softly wept, he held her in his arms, murmuring words of hope. At last the pretty blonde looked into Beaumont's dark eyes and asked, "If we make it through this awful ordeal, will we see each other again?"

Although not wanting to give Becky Sue false expectations, he did not have the heart to reject her when she was so vulnerable. He gave her a reassuring smile and drawled, "Why of course we'll see each other again."

She smiled happily, and the Southerner was quite disconcerted when she leaned up and kissed him softly. "Thank you for being so considerate," she murmured. Then she settled back in his arms again.

There was intermittent gunfire from both sides of the river during the morning, but no one was hit. Apparently Three Hands merely wanted his quarry to know he was still there and he was going to wait them out. It would be a simple matter. He had food; they did not.

Midafternoon, Clete Holman came upon Todd Dressler talking to Alf Kyle in the brush on the north side of the island. Kyle was clearly verging on panic. Dressler, who was holding a canteen, was assuring his friend that everything was going to turn out all right. "You need to put more water in your stomach; then you'll feel better," the ex-corporal announced. "I'll go fill it."

As Dressler turned away, Holman stopped him and asked, "What's the matter?"

"He's just got the jitters. Stay with him till I get back, okay?"

"Sure. But before you go, answer one thing for me," he demanded, looking the former soldier in the eye. "You're not gonna give up your gun to Lonegan when this thing's over, are you?"

"Not on your life," Dressler retorted. Then he headed off, saying, "I'll be right back."

He headed for a spot where some thick bushes hung over the water in the shade of the dense trees, where the people knew they could fill the canteens without exposing themselves to the Dog Men marksmen. Carrying a Spencer in one hand, Dressler was almost at the spot when he saw a Cheyenne warrior crawling onto the island out of the underbrush, dripping wet. Startled, he dropped the canteen and brought up the rifle, hollering, "Hey!"

The swift hand of the Indian hurled a knife with lightning speed. There was a brief glint of light from the blade in the mottled sunlight before it pierced Dressler's bare chest all the way to the haft.

The smirk of triumph on the Cheyenne's face was quickly replaced with fear as Clete Holman abruptly appeared. Holman's rifle immediately boomed, and the warrior fell dead.

Most of the islanders came rushing to the spot. Lowering his smoking rifle, Holman told them, "If there were more, I didn't see 'em."

"I am certain he was alone," spoke up Little Star. "Three Hands sent him as a spy to find out how many of us are left. He has no way of knowing the effect his rain of arrows had."

Suddenly Alf Kyle elbowed his way past the circle of people, stopping dead in his tracks when he saw Todd Dressler's lifeless body. Dropping to his knees, he shook the corpse, shouting, "No, you can't leave me! Please!"

Touching his shoulder, Vint Lonegan said, "Come on, Kyle. We need to put his body with the others."

Alf Kyle's eyes took on a wild look. Shaking his fists, he screamed, "We'll never get off this island alive! We'll slowly starve to death or be picked off one by one." His screaming became incoherent, and saliva sprayed from his mouth.

Vint Lonegan gripped one of his arms and stung his face with two open-handed blows, saying, "Get ahold of yourself, man!" The screaming stopped, and Kyle looked at Lonegan as though he were seeing him for the first time. The wild look in his eyes faded, and the captain asked, "Are you all right now?"

Kyle blinked, nodding his head. "Yeah. Yeah, I'm all right."

Out on the plains, Three Hands grew impatient as the sun lowered on the western horizon. He had heard the single shot fired on the island earlier, and when his spy never returned, the subchief was sure the warrior had been caught and killed.

Although he was anxious to get on with his scheme to kill the old chief and take over the tribe, he had to have the Spencer repeaters in his hands. Figuring his own numbers would be quickly reduced if they rushed the island, he decided to try negotiating with the whites. If the trick worked, he could kill everyone on the island and take his rifles. If not, he would force himself to remain patient and starve them out.

Taking two warriors with him, one of whom had a white cloth tied to his rifle, Three Hands walked toward the river. The soldier on duty at the south side of the island saw the trio approaching the bank of the river, and he called to Three Hands to speak.

The subchief asked to confer with their leader, and the soldier disappeared into the brush to summon him.

Three Hands was disappointed when Vint Lonegan appeared.

"What do you want?" Lonegan shouted across the water.

Replying firmly, the Cheyenne declared, "I have come to offer you a chance to live!"

"I'm listening!"

"We have plenty of food. You face death by starvation. I give you my word that if you give us the rifles and ammunition, I will let you live. No one will be harmed. You can all go free."

Suddenly Little Star stepped out of the brush and stood beside Vint Lonegan. Her hands on her hips, she yelled heatedly, "You lie, Three Hands! You know Vint Lonegan heard your plan to murder my father! You plan to kill us all, no matter what we do—just as you are planning to kill Burning Sun!"

Lonegan called, "We will take a vote among us. However the vote goes, that is what we will do!"

The captain then turned to the people massed behind him and conferred with them. Only a few moments had passed when he faced Three Hands once again. "We just took a vote, and we are all in agreement: If the mighty Three Hands wants the rifles, you'll have to come and take them!"

The subchief's face darkened with rage. He would not be satisfied until these men—and the woman who had spurned him—were all dead. Turning from the riverbank, his eyes blazing, he strode angrily back to his camp.

Night came, and the hunger of those on the island was becoming unbearable. As they sat around the fire, Alf Kyle was quivering and showing signs of breaking. Vint Lonegan left the fire and took Kyle into the brush to talk to him alone. As soon as Lonegan was gone, Clete Holman stared lustfully at Little Star, but she ignored him and stared into the flames.

When Lonegan and Kyle returned, the deserter was quiet. He sat down next to Mickey Wilson, pulled his knees up, and buried his face against them. Holman looked at the captain, nodded toward Kyle, and asked, "Is he gonna be okay?"

Lonegan merely shrugged.

Sometime during the middle of the night, Holman awakened suddenly. Lifting his head, he looked around and saw that Alf Kyle, who had been sleeping beside him, was gone. Then he heard the bushes rustle and realized Kyle's movement through the brush was what had awakened him. Seconds later, Holman thought he heard a dull splash, but when all was quiet after that, he went back to sleep.

Rising at dawn, Holman noticed that Kyle was still not in his bedroll. The gunrunner automatically grabbed his rifle as he got up. Then he walked toward Vint Lonegan, Lieutenant Beaumont, and Little Star, who were standing near the south edge of the island looking across the river to the mainland. Calling to them, he asked, "Any of you seen Alf?"

Lonegan threw him a strained look and muttered, "I'm afraid so."

A chill slithered down his spine, and Holman ran to where they stood and peered through the brush. His eyes bulged at what he saw. There on the far bank was Alf Kyle, standing naked and impaled on a long stake. His arms hanging limply at his sides and his head lolling loosely, like a doll with a broken neck, Kyle sagged against the stake with blood running from his right breast down his body. It was obvious that he was barely clinging to life.

Holman gasped, "He's alive!"

"Unfortunately," Lonegan responded. "I guess he slipped away during the night thinking he could elude the Dog Men and swim to freedom." He sighed, adding, "I warned him if he tried to escape, they'd catch him. I guess his desperation won out over his good sense."

Hearing the voices, Kyle lifted his head with obvious great effort and looked across the river at the small group. "Please," he groaned, his words riding on the still air, "please kill me."

Little Star gripped Lonegan's arm, her nails biting into the skin. "O, Heammawihio," she breathed shakily, "let him die!"

"Please," Kyle repeated. "Somebody . . . kill me."

Sweating, Clete Holman levered a cartridge into the chamber of his rifle, shouldered it, and, taking careful aim, pressed the trigger. The report of the rifle frightened a flock of magpies, and they fluttered instantly from their roost on the island. Alf Kyle jerked with the impact of the bullet as it pierced his heart, and then his body sagged lifelessly against the stake. The spectators stood in silence for a long moment and then slowly turned. The others came on the run and were told what had happened. Then all of them headed quietly back toward the clearing.

The bodies at the west end of the island were beginning to smell, and everyone agreed they had no choice but to throw them in the river. While the men went to perform their odious task, Little Star left her tending of Harley Carter—whose leg wound had become infected, making him very fevered—and took Becky Sue Moore to the other end of the island so she would not have to see her sister's body floating away. Clete Holman stayed behind, saying he would take over Little Star's ministrations and bathe Harley Carter's fevered face with cool water.

After a few minutes, Becky Sue told Little Star that she wanted to be alone for a while, so the maiden headed back to the clearing. Suddenly she found herself face to face with Clete Holman. Looking past him to the clearing, she saw Harley Carter lying alone; the rest of the men were still at the end of the island.

Holman showed his mouthful of yellow teeth in a lascivious grin. "I think it's time," he told her in a low voice.

"For what?" she asked.

"For this," he said, grabbing her by the arms and planting a fierce, hungry kiss on her lips.

Little Star pushed against him with all her strength, but he held her tight. She squealed and struggled like an animal in a trap, and finally breaking his hold, she slapped his face violently.

Just then the three officers stepped into the clearing from the other direction. With a roar, Vint Lonegan charged the gunrunner like an enraged bull. Little Star stepped out of his way, spitting and wiping her mouth as though she had eaten something foul. Turning, Holman's eyes widened and he braced himself, clawing for his revolver.

But Holman was too slow. The furious captain sent a vicious punch to his jaw, lifting the outlaw off his feet. Knocked unconscious by the blow, Holman slithered to the ground and lay in a crumpled heap.

As Lonegan took Little Star in his arms, William Louis Beaumont shook his head admiringly and said, "I do declare, Captain Lonegan, you pack a potent punch! You remind me of a mule we once had who used to knock the barn door down with a single kick!"

Lonegan grinned and quipped, "First I remind you of your grandmother, then your cousin. Now it's a mule you used to have. Well, like I said before, at least you're keeping it in the family!"

Everyone had a good laugh, while Beaumont feigned anger and muttered to himself. Then his face, too, split into a grin. It felt good to laugh—even if just for a moment.

When Clete Holman regained consciousness, his holster was empty. Vint Lonegan informed him he was not to have a gun any longer and warned him if he touched Little Star again, he would kill him. Holman would tend to Harley Carter and fetch water—nothing more.

Swearing angrily to himself, the gunrunner got up and went back to the clearing. But it was evident from the look in his eyes that Captain Vint Lonegan was his enemy.

Beaumont stepped beside Lonegan and his face darkened. "Let me have him, Vint. We don't have much of a chance anyway, so let me get revenge for what he did to Art Sands."

Shaking his head, the captain responded, "I can't let you do that, Beau. As an officer in the United States Army, you'd be guilty of murder. If we were to get off this island, you'd face a firing squad."

The Southerner gritted his teeth. "It'd almost be worth it."

Chapter Twelve

Night fell yet again. Everyone on the island was starving, but no one mentioned food, and attempting to distract themselves, they all busied themselves as best they could.

Two of the troopers were on watch, while another one stood guard over the rifles, ensuring that Clete Holman did not arm himself. William Louis Beaumont and Becky Sue Moore strolled through the brush, talking, while Little Star stood with Vint Lonegan at the east end of the island as he and Lieutenant Carl Clendennan debated what to do if no one came from Fort McPherson.

While the captain and the lieutenant talked on, Little Star wandered idly through the trees and shortly found herself near the clearing, where Clete Holman sat alone with Harley Carter. Unnoticed by either man, the maiden stood in the bushes and heard Holman cursing Vint Lonegan for denying him a gun. Chuckling evilly, the gunrunner shared with his cohort that he had a double-barreled derringer hidden under his belt. He was saving one bullet for Lonegan and the other for Beaumont, who seemed to have something against him. He could feel the Southerner's eyes boring into him frequently, and when he met the man's gaze, he could practically feel his rage. Then Holman added that even if the man did not have a grudge against him, just being Lonegan's friend was enough to seal his fate. When things got to where they looked hopeless—when it no longer mattered to keep them alive and aid his own survival—Holman would save the Dog Men the trouble of killing those two.

Little Star slipped away, cold sweat on her brow. She was afraid to tell Lonegan about the derringer, for Holman was a desperate man—and the captain could get killed trying to take the gun away from him. The maiden decided she would find a way to get the derringer from Clete Holman herself.

Dawn brought renewed hunger and noticeable weakness to the besieged prisoners. It was all too evident that no help was coming from Fort McPherson, and Lonegan and Clendennan had been unable to come up with a plan of escape from the island—without everyone ending up as Alf Kyle had.

The men had scraggly beards, and everyone's eyes were dull and their faces drawn. Harley Carter was now delirious with fever.

Sitting slightly apart from the others, Beaumont and Becky Sue were talking softly with each other as they sipped their morning ration of water. In a low voice, the pretty blonde took hold of the Frenchman's hand and said, "Beau, I see nothing but despair on everyone's face, and it's clear that we're not going to get off this island alive. So I want to say something to you before it's too late. I—"

Beaumont put a finger to her lips and said, "Don't talk that way. We'll make it somehow."

"Please," she insisted, looking deeply into his eyes, "let me say it."

He nodded.

"I love you, Beau," she whispered, her voice breaking. "I felt something special for you the moment we boarded the stage, and spending all this time together has made me realize how deeply I care for you."

Blushing, the Southerner protested, "Becky Sue . . ."

"I wouldn't be so bold if the circumstances were different," she admitted. "I love you with everything that is in me, and when I want to block this horrid nightmare out of my mind for a few moments, I think of what it would be like if you were in love with me, and . . . and if things were normal and I could be your wife. Oh, Beau, nothing would make me happier than to hear you say that you love me, too."

William Louis Beaumont swallowed hard. He half choked as he said, "Becky Sue, I—"

Suddenly a sentry's voice cut the morning air from the south side of the island. "Grab your guns! The Indians are splitting into two groups and they're going to attack from both sides!"

Cursing as he stood up, Beaumont declared, "Three Hands knows how weakened we are by now. I'll give him this: He's calculated his move perfectly." He then ran and took his position. Becky Sue insisted on going with him, wanting to remain beside the man she loved and use a rifle as best she could. Rather than argue, the Southerner said, "We need all the firepower we can muster."

Three Hands apparently gave the signal to charge, for suddenly dozens of pinto ponies plunged into the river and guns blazed. The subchief remained on his horse near the bank of the river and watched, his face smug, clearly assuming the battle would last only a few minutes. But the Dog Men soon found that their prisoners were still alert and strong enough to squeeze triggers and reload rifles and withstand the assault.

While the battle raged, one warrior left his horse unnoticed and got onto the island. Becky Sue Moore and William Louis Beaumont were on their knees, blasting away at the far shore. When Becky Sue used her last shot, she turned to pick up a loaded rifle.

The Indian was standing a few yards behind them, drawing a bead on Beaumont. Spotting him, she screamed, "Beau!" The Southerner started to turn to see what she was warning him about when she leapt in front of him, shielding him.

The Indian's rifle barked and the slug ripped into the blonde's chest. Dropping his single-shot rifle, the warrior pulled his knife. But Beaumont had shouldered his repeater and he fired, dropping the Cheyenne.

Letting his own rifle fall to the ground, Beaumont knelt beside the young woman and saw that she was still breathing. "Oh, Becky Sue!" he wailed. "You deliberately took that bullet for me! You saved my life!"

Blood was spreading rapidly on the front of her dress as he picked her up and carried her to the clearing. He could tell from where the Cheyenne bullet had entered her chest just above her heart that she would not live much longer.

Three Hands was enraged as he saw his men going down under the guns of the besieged people on the island. Bloodied, terrified pintos were bounding out of the river onto the banks as their lifeless riders floated eastward on the current. Raising his rifle, the subchief shouted above the din for his men to retreat. Word passed quickly among the braves, and the warriors who remained headed out of rifle range.

The firing on the island stopped. Moments later, the Dog Men were gathering around their leader as he sat on his horse, counting his losses. Suddenly Three Hands saw Vint Lonegan appear at the edge of the island with Little Star by his side. The big muscular captain was looking at him with defiance. Unable to contain his wrath any more, Three Hands ripped off his headdress and threw it on the ground. His eyes blazing, he kicked his pony's sides and raced into the river.

Seeing him coming, Vint Lonegan peeled off his shirt and laid down his rifle and then stepped into the water.

"Vint!" Little Star gasped. "You are too weak from hunger to fight him! He will kill you!"

"We'll see about that!" he called confidently over his shoulder.

The warrior was halfway to the island when his horse suddenly lurched to one side. Grabbing for the animal's mane to stay on his back, Three Hands dropped his prized nickel-plated Spencer into the river. But he kept going, determined to meet his mortal enemy in combat. Grinning menacingly, he shrieked, "I do not need a weapon to take your puny life, white-eyes pig!"

Lonegan yelled, "Suits me fine! I can think of nothing more pleasurable than killing an insane beast like you with my own two hands!"

The two combatants met in the middle of the river between island and prairie, and Three Hands leapt off his horse onto his opponent. They immediately locked in struggle, and the Indian was surprised by the strength and ferocity of the captain. It was more than he had anticipated—much more. He was astounded that someone who had gone so long without food could have so much strength.

Three Hands felt himself being lifted out of the water and then plunged straight down like a pole. His feet struck the rocky bottom hard, shooting streamers of pain through his legs.

The traitor came up spewing water and threw an arm around Lonegan's neck, dragging him under. Water bubbled and foamed as they fought; then suddenly both men broke the surface, with the captain's neck still locked in the crook of the strong subchief's arm and the subchief attempting to cut off the air from his windpipe. Lonegan drove an elbow into the Indian's rib cage with such force that it knocked the wind from his lungs, and he let go.

Jumping onto the Cheyenne, Lonegan pulled him under again, and the two men plunged to the rocky bed of the river, grappling for a long moment. Then the combatants shot up out of the water and Lonegan drove another stiff punch to the red man's jaw. Three Hands fell backward, and the captain was on him again.

The words of one of the warriors on the south bank drifted across the water: "I must help Three Hands!"

But one of the other braves yelled, "No, you must not! You would bring great shame to the mighty Three Hands if you went to his rescue. Even if Three Hands should be killed by the white man, he must die in honor. If you help, it would dishonor him."

Three Hands was again driven to the bottom of the North Platte by his powerful opponent, but this time he came up with his knife in his right hand, the blade flashing in the sun. The subchief had discovered that he could not kill Vint Lonegan without a weapon after all.

Three Hands was fast. Before Lonegan could grasp the wrist of the knife hand, the Cheyenne swung the deadly blade. But the slippery rocks under his feet spoiled his aim, and instead of driving the blade into the white man's heart, it slashed Lonegan's left shoulder. Blood spurted from the wound, but still Lonegan did not pull his own knife. He clearly was bent on killing the traitor with his bare hands.

Three Hands tried to swing the knife again, but the angered captain seized the wrist and they locked nose to nose. "You die!" breathed the Indian hotly.

"Not today!" countered the muscular white man.

With a surge of power, Lonegan savagely twisted the wrist that held the knife, and Three Hands howled in pain. Prying the weapon loose, Lonegan threw it downriver, and it quickly disappeared under the surface.

Getting the upper hand, the powerful subchief

grabbed Lonegan around the throat, driving his head
under the water. The captain rallied his strength and
fought violently, finally succeeding in breaking free. He
came up sputtering and coughing, gasping for air. Grinning victoriously, Three Hands knelt slightly, ready to
spring out of the water onto his enemy. But before the
Indian could complete his move, Lonegan sank his fingers into his long black hair and viciously snapped his
head back, pulling him unexpectedly beneath the surface so that the Indian swallowed a great deal of water.
The subchief fought for all he was worth, thrashing
furiously and putting up a tremendous battle. Bubbles
and foam rose to the top, floating away on the lazy
current.

The Cheyenne's strength was waning. Wanting to
prolong the traitor's agony, Lonegan let him up, and
when Three Hands surfaced, his face had taken on a
slightly blue hue. Blood was pumping from his nose and
mouth, and as he gasped, coughed, and choked, he
sprayed his opponent with blood and water.

Finally the captain hissed, "Good-bye, mighty
Three Hands!" and pushed him under the surface
again.

The dying man kicked and fought hard, trying to
break Lonegan's viselike grip. His eyes bulged from
their sockets, looking up at his white enemy through
the crystal-clear water, and the knowledge of death was
in them.

The warrior's struggle for life went on for another
two minutes. Then, his lungs filling with water, his body
went limp.

Releasing his enemy, Captain Vint Lonegan
straightened up, breathing hard, and watched the lifeless corpse bob to the surface and float downstream like
a chunk of flotsam. Then he looked across to the shoreline at the Dog Men, who stood mute, watching their
leader drift away on the current. He knew they would
launch a ferocious attack on the islanders in retribution

for Three Hands's death—and the survivors had better prepare for it.

Exhausted and losing blood from his shoulder wound, the captain stumbled through the waist-deep water toward the island, where Little Star and most of the others were waiting. While everyone else cheered Lonegan, congratulating him on his victory, the Cheyenne maiden embraced him with tears flowing down her cheeks, cautioning, "We must stop the bleeding quickly."

As the group returned to the clearing, they discovered William Louis Beaumont sitting on the ground, holding a dying Becky Sue in his arms. Blood was spread completely across the front of her dress, and she was unconscious, although the pain showed on her face.

Little Star gasped, "What happened?"

"She was shot by one of the Dog Men. He sneaked on the island durin' the fightin', and he would have killed me—except Becky Sue leapt in front of me and took the bullet instead," the Southerner replied sorrowfully. "I fear that she's mortally wounded."

Kneeling, Little Star examined Becky Sue's wound. Her eyes met Beaumont's, and she nodded sadly. Clearly there was nothing they could do for her.

The maiden then turned to Lonegan and told him to sit. She immediately went to work on the gash on his shoulder.

Suddenly Becky Sue moaned and her eyes fluttered open. Cradled in the arms of the man she loved, she looked up at the handsome Frenchman and said weakly, "Beau?"

"Yes?" he replied tenderly.

"You . . . you were about to tell me something . . . when the Indians came. Was . . . was it that you . . . love me?"

Beaumont's eyes misted as he looked into the dying face of the sweet, innocent girl who had purposely taken a Cheyenne bullet to save his life. "Yes, Becky

Sue," he murmured softly, "I love you. I love you more than I could ever tell you."

The pretty blonde smiled through her pain. Beaumont bent down and kissed her forehead, his tears falling onto her face. She raised a weak hand and lovingly touched his cheek. "I . . . I wish I could have become your wife."

Wiping the tears from his face, the man from New Orleans looked over at Lieutenant Carl Clendennan, who stood nearby. "Lieutenant . . ."

Clendennan came over and knelt down beside them. "Yes?"

"In the Confederate Army, an officer could perform a weddin' if a chaplain wasn't available," Beaumont stated. "Is it the same in the Union Army?"

"Sure is," Clendennan confirmed with a nod, looking with compassion at the dying young woman.

"Would . . . would you marry Becky Sue and me? Right now, I mean?" He looked down at the blonde in his arms. "That is, if she'll have me."

"Oh, Beau!" Becky Sue exclaimed weakly. "Yes . . . yes I will!"

Foregoing any lengthy words or repetition of vows, the lieutenant conducted a brief ceremony and then pronounced them husband and wife. Tears sprang into his own eyes as he told Beaumont, "You may kiss your bride."

The Southerner smiled sweetly at the young woman, who looked up at him with adoration and joy. Bending his head, he whispered, "I love you, my darlin'," then kissed her.

While they kissed, the life left Becky Sue's body. Beaumont stiffened, and with tears streaming down his face, he straightened up. Cradling her head lovingly on his lap, he just stared at her face, which was peaceful now and had a look of happiness.

After a few minutes, Little Star went to him and put a hand on his shoulder. "That was a beautiful thing you did," she whispered hoarsely, "marrying Becky Sue so she could die happy and content."

Beaumont looked up at her and blinked against his tears, shaking his head sadly. "I did not marry her out of gratitude or out of pity, Little Star. I realized at the moment she saved my life that—" his voice broke "—that I loved her."

Little Star stared into his eyes for a long moment, then touched his cheek gently. Silently, she returned to Vint Lonegan and finished tending his wound.

While she was doing so, Clete Holman came over to them and bent down. "Captain, you've got to let me handle a gun," he told Lonegan. "Those savages are gonna come back. You know it, and I know it."

Little Star glanced at him, seeing under his belt the pearl handle of the derringer. Remembering that he planned to kill Lonegan and Beaumont when the situation looked hopeless, she realized she had to get the gun from him soon.

Before Lonegan could answer the gunrunner, one of the troopers stepped up and said, "Captain, Dressler's buddy Mickey Wilson was killed in this last attack. He's over on the north side." Looking at Holman, the young soldier added, "And you might want to know that your pal Harley Carter's dead, too."

When the young man returned to his post, Lonegan looked at Clete Holman and said, "You'll get no gun. You're the last of the outlaw bunch, and the rest of us know what you would do if you had a gun. I'm warning you: Try anything, and one of us will kill you."

"But listen, Lonegan," argued Holman, "I've got a right to—"

"Gunrunners don't have any rights!" Lonegan countered. "Besides, the situation is futile. There's no way we can repel another attack. The next one will be the last."

A black shroud seemed to hover over the island. Everyone knew they were doomed. Little Star finished knotting the bandage and Lonegan stood up. Taking a deep breath, he looked around at the survivors—consisting of himself, Little Star, Beaumont, Clendennan, Holman, and two troopers—and said, "The Cheyenne will no doubt attack at any time. We all saw it in their faces. Since this will surely be our last stand, I suggest that each of you take time to pray alone if you so desire."

The captain stared intently at Clete Holman and then asked, "Tell me something, Holman. Do you still think selling guns to the Indians is a good idea?"

The outlaw was silent.

"Just out of curiosity," Lonegan continued, "who is your supplier?"

Shrugging, Holman said, "Well, I guess it don't matter none to tell you now. After all, there's no way you're gonna get off this island alive." With a glint in his eye, the gunrunner revealed the name and whereabouts of his supplier to Vint Lonegan, and then turned away.

Little Star saw the look in Clete Holman's eyes and knew he was going to make his move soon. The maiden realized she might have to watch the man she loved die —but it was not going to be at the hands of Clete Holman.

As the group solemnly dispersed, she told Lonegan that she wanted a moment alone also. He nodded and then knelt down to help Beaumont carry Becky Sue's body into the bushes.

Reaching the edge of the clearing, Little Star brushed past Clete Holman, who stood watching Lonegan. She gave him a provocative glance, whispering, "Follow me."

Clearly startled, Holman eagerly complied. They headed through the brush, and when they were alone, Little Star fought the revulsion she felt toward Holman and whispered, "I must tell you the truth. I am very attracted to you. I could not let on about this because of Vint. But since we are soon to die when the Dog Men attack, it makes no difference now if the truth is known."

Clete Holman was obviously taken totally by surprise. Smiling lustfully, he grinned, showing his yellow teeth. "I understand, little beauty."

The maiden put her arms around the outlaw's waist, pulling him closer. Looking into his cruel face, she breathed, "I could not face what is coming without having the chance to be with you."

Holman's eyes were wild with passion, and he licked his lips in anticipation. Little Star felt her stomach turn as she kissed the outlaw lingeringly on his repulsive mouth. At the same time, her right hand moved toward his midsection. Clete Holman was clearly too consumed by lust to feel her hand until her finger had closed on the derringer under his belt. Then, suddenly aware of what was happening, he broke off the kiss, swearing angrily, and reached for the gun.

But it was too late.

Little Star pressed the muzzle to his stomach and fired the derringer. His hand had already seized her wrist, but when the slug tore into his body, his mouth flew open from the impact and he let go as he buckled violently. Little Star took two steps back, holding the small gun leveled on him. Hurried footsteps were coming through the brush behind her.

The shocked outlaw held one hand over the bleeding hole in his belly and staggered forward, reaching for the woman with the other hand. His eyes were crazed. Little Star took two more backward steps as Holman cried wordlessly and lunged at her, and she fired again at his chest.

Vint Lonegan and William Louis Beaumont broke through the heavy foliage in time to see Clete Holman fall dead. Little Star turned and looked at Lonegan, dropped the smoking derringer, and dashed into his arms.

"Oh, Vint!" she gasped. "He had the gun under his

belt. I overheard him tell Harley Carter he was going to kill you and Beau with it!"

As Lonegan held her tight, he asked, "Honey, why didn't you tell me about it? I'd have taken it away from him."

"He might have shot you when you tried," she replied. "I had to kiss his foul mouth to get the gun, but at least you will not die by his wicked hand!"

Shaking his head in amazement, Lonegan told her, "You sure are some courageous woman!"

Beaumont stepped beside her, declaring, "I second that thought. You have my gratitude, Little Star."

Suddenly Lieutenant Clendennan's voice cut the air. "Captain Lonegan! They're coming!"

They hurried through the brush to the edge of the island and looked southward at the mainland. Standing on the riverbank in front of Alf Kyle's body, which was still impaled on the stake, were the Dog Men warriors with lances in their hands and knives between their teeth. In the middle of the warriors, wearing Three Hands's long headdress, was their new leader, who stood proudly among his braves.

Little Star gripped Vint Lonegan's arm as he advised, "This is it. They're going to come onto the island for a hand-to-hand battle to the end. We'll get a few when they charge across the river, but there's no way we're going to get all of them. We'd better get ready."

Bellying down shoulder to shoulder on the island's south bank, the weary, besieged survivors took up rifles and braced themselves for the attack.

Lieutenant Clendennan broke the ominous silence, saying fervently, "It's been a real honor to know all of you. Too bad it has to come to this kind of an end."

"It's better this way than slowly starving to death," muttered Beaumont.

Lonegan turned to his friend lying beside him on the left. The two men looked at each for a long moment but found no words. The captain then turned to Little

Star lying on his right and told her softly, "I love you, darling."

The Indian maiden's eyes were swimming in tears. "And I love you," she choked.

They kissed tenderly, knowing it would be the last time. Then they waited for death to claim their love.

Suddenly a heavy rumbling noise came drifting across the North Platte River from the north. At first it sounded like thunder, but it quickly became recognizable as pounding hooves. Then hundreds of howling Cheyenne massed over the gentle slopes, galloping toward the river.

The people on the island all stood, dumbfounded, as Chief Burning Sun's faithful Hotamitanui warriors raced like a stampeding herd of buffalo, rifles blazing as they fired at the men on the shore. Three Hands's traitorous followers began screaming and diving into the river as the riders charged directly toward them. Reining in their mounts at the water's edge, they continued shooting at their fleeing brothers.

Amid screams, gunfire, and smoke, all the traitors were dead within less than five minutes. Their bloody bodies could be seen floating down the river as the smoke began to clear.

When the battle ended, the mounted warriors formed themselves into ranks on the riverbank. Suddenly Little Star gasped, for riding slowly from the rear, between an opening in the middle of the ranks, was the stately chief of the Hotamitanui band. His full headdress gleamed in the bright sunlight, and the tip of his ceremonial spear shone. Halting at the shoreline, he looked across to the island and then beckoned his daughter to come to him.

Little Star looked up at Vint Lonegan, who told her, "Go to your father."

Burning Sun dismounted and stood watching her the whole time while the beautiful maiden swam across the river. When she reached the other side, he held out his arms, and she rushed into them. He embraced her for a long moment and then held her at arm's length. Speaking softly, he asked, "Can my daughter ever forgive her father for his blind foolishness?"

"Blind foolishness, father?" she said, her heart pounding.

"Yes. These old eyes were too blind to see Three Hands for what he really was—a snake-bellied traitor."

"Father," she gasped with surprise, "how do you know of Three Hands's treachery? How did you know to come here?"

"It was Hungry Wolf," replied the old man. "I sent him with Three Hands to bring you back—but he learned that Three Hands planned to murder me and take over our tribe. Hungry Wolf tried to rise up against him, but Three Hands shot him and had his men throw him into the river."

Little Star's face reflected her confusion. "Then how—"

"Three Hands only thought Hungry Wolf was dead," answered the weathered chief. "But he came out of the river and managed to take one of the ponies. He rode to camp and lived long enough to tell me of Three Hands's plan." He paused, then added, "We will give Hungry Wolf a hero's burial."

Looking deeply into her father's eyes, Little Star told him, "I think we should thank Heammawihio for helping Hungry Wolf make it to the camp."

Burning Sun nodded. Then, looking uncomfortable and clearing his throat, he told her, "I was wrong for sending Captain Vint Lonegan away and for trying to force you to marry Three Hands. There are no words to express my regret. But I must know: Will my daughter forgive her foolish father?"

The lovely maiden embraced her father tightly. "Yes, my father. Oh, yes, I forgive you."

Burning Sun's stern face softened. "I am much

pleased. But I must also ask forgiveness from Vint Lonegan."

Little Star turned and motioned for the rest of the survivors to come across. Lonegan immediately waded into the river, making his way ahead of the others. While Lonegan was crossing, Little Star asked, "Father, did you notice that Three Hands was not among the warriors your men just killed?"

"I did notice," the old man replied with a nod.

"That is because Vint killed him with his bare hands earlier this morning," she explained. "Drowned him in the river."

Leaving her father's side, the young maiden went to Lonegan as he stepped ashore. Taking him by the hand, she excitedly led him to where her father stood, explaining how Burning Sun and his warriors came to be there.

Lonegan smiled gratefully at the chief and took the hand offered to him. Burning Sun's dark eyes regarded the captain, and then he declared, "Vint Lonegan, your people have a saying: There is no fool like an old fool. This chief has been such a fool. Fortunately his blinded eyes were opened before it was too late."

"I am glad for you, sir." Then he grinned, adding, "I am glad for *all* of us."

"I would ask your forgiveness," the old man said with feeling.

Lonegan clasped the old man's hand firmly. "The mighty Chief Burning Sun has my forgiveness."

"My daughter tells me that I am in your debt for killing the viper, Three Hands. How can I repay you?"

Flicking a glance at Little Star, Lonegan replied, "By giving me your daughter's hand in marriage."

A slow smile spread across Burning Sun's lined old face. He reached up and put his hand on the white man's muscular shoulder, declaring, "It shall be so."

Little Star threw her arms around her father's waist. "Oh, thank you, my father! Thank you!"

The old chief regarded them fondly. "When would you like to be married?"

Lonegan looked at the maiden and then back at Burning Sun. "We need a few days to recuperate from this ordeal. How about a week from today? I would like to get the chaplain here from Fort McPherson, if possible."

"One week from today it shall be," agreed Burning Sun. "Let us all now return to our camp. We will have a feast and fatten you all back up."

A week later, excitement was in the air as the whole encampment made preparations for the wedding. Colonel Donald Harrington had come, along with the fort chaplain. To help make the surviving soldiers more presentable, he had brought spare uniforms, razors, and soap, and as a gift to the groom, he gave Captain Vint Lonegan some toilet water.

Preparing for the wedding ceremony in one of the tepees, Lonegan finished shaving and slapped the strong-smelling toilet water on his face. He was glad Lieutenant Clendennan, Corporal Slate, and Trooper Ed Yancey had stayed on for the wedding. He was even more pleased to have Lieutenant William Louis Beaumont for his best man, although he felt a twinge of sorrow for Beaumont's loss of Becky Sue. At least she had been given a decent burial at the Cheyenne camp by Burning Sun's people.

Suddenly the flap came open and the Frenchman entered. "Well, you sure look better with a shave," Lonegan declared.

Twitching his nose, Beaumont sniffed twice and then exclaimed, "Whew! What do I smell?"

"That's my new toilet water," Lonegan replied, laughing. "Colonel Harrington gave it to me for a wedding present."

Chuckling, Beaumont said, "You remind me of a skunk I once—"

Almost before the words were off his tongue, the Southerner grinned. Slapping a palm to his forehead, he joined Lonegan as they said in unison, *"At least you're keeping it in the family!"*

The wedding ceremony was brief but moving, with Vint Lonegan and Little Star taking their vows first in the Cheyenne tradition and then in front of the fort chaplain. Afterward, there was a great feast, and giggling with pleasure as they ate side by side, Little Star remarked to her new husband, "Now I finally understand when you told me to save those words."

Lonegan looked at her with puzzlement.

"Don't you remember?" she chided. "You told me to save the words, 'I do,' because you had a better use for them." She giggled again. "And you did."

Later that evening, under the light of the moon, William Louis Beaumont and the five soldiers made ready to leave. Colonel Harrington and his men would return to the fort, but Beaumont had resigned his commission. He would ride with the soldiers as far as North Platte and then head home to New Orleans, with a brief stop in Kansas to locate Becky Sue and Patty Moore's parents and tell them of the tragedy. Vint Lonegan and his new bride would follow the soldiers in a few days, at which time they would take up residence at Fort McPherson—although the captain would then immediately go after Clete Holman's supplier.

The men came to give their best wishes to the bride and groom. The last to do so, Corporal Will Slate shook hands with Lonegan and then stepped close to the bride and said, "Little Star, I hope your husband won't mind, but I just wanted to tell you that you're the most beautiful woman I have ever seen—and the bravest. It was a real privilege to fight alongside you."

Lonegan smiled proudly as Little Star thanked him and then planted a kiss on his cheek. Slate blinked with surprise, grinned sheepishly, and hurried to his horse.

Beaumont stepped in front of the couple and smiled warmly at them. Kissing Little Star's cheek, he told her, "When I start my new Confederate Army, I want you to be my general in charge of marksmanship."

Little Star laughed and replied, "Only if my husband will let me!"

"Not a chance," Lonegan quippped, and then offered his hand to his friend. His face suddenly solemn and wistful, he said, "I hope you come back and see us soon, my good friend."

"You can count on it," drawled the man from New Orleans, gripping Lonegan's hand hard.

The men mounted up and headed southward along the bank of the Blue River, leaving Lonegan and Little Star standing arm in arm, waving to them. After riding about fifty yards, Beaumont reined in and looked back at the newlyweds, who were enjoying a long, rapturous kiss.

Corporal Slate nudged his horse close to the Southerner and sighed, "Golly, Beau, wouldn't you like to be doing that?"

William Louis Beaumont chuckled and replied, "I admit I'm fond of Captain Lonegan—but I wouldn't want to kiss him, even in the moonlight!"

Laughing heartily, the men turned their horses and road off into the night.

STAGECOACH STATION 47:
JUÁREZ
by Hank Mitchum

In May 1893, at the conclusion of successful talks between the United States and Mexico, Secretary of War Duncan Campbell and his family prepare to leave Juárez, Mexico, and return to Washington. But their plans are abruptly altered when they are kidnapped and held hostage by Guatemalan guerrillas, hoping to gain the release of their countrymen arrested for murder in Louisiana.

When federal officials learn that Campbell, his wife, and beautiful daughter, Lucy, are being held by a fierce guerrilla leader in a heavily guarded mansion near Chihuahua, they send for United States Marshal John McCain, one of the best young lawmen in the country. Aided by a band of Mexican patriots, McCain plots a daring rescue, full of intrigue and suspense. After a vicious battle—in which he is nearly taken captive himself—McCain manages to free the hostages. But their troubles are not over yet.

During a desperate race across Mexico by stagecoach, the lawman and young Lucy Campbell are drawn together by a powerful magnetism. But the journey to safety is an arduous and treacherous one, and the travelers are repeatedly endangered, making McCain and Lucy wonder if they will survive the obstacles that threaten their growing love—and, indeed, their very lives.

Read JUÁREZ, on sale May 1990 wherever Bantam paperbacks are sold.

★ WAGONS WEST ★

This continuing, magnificent saga recounts the adventures of a brave band of settlers, all of different backgrounds, all sharing one dream—to find a new and better life.

☐	26822	**INDEPENDENCE! #1**	$4.50
☐	26162	**NEBRASKA! #2**	$4.50
☐	26242	**WYOMING! #3**	$4.50
☐	26072	**OREGON! #4**	$4.50
☐	26070	**TEXAS! #5**	$4.50
☐	26377	**CALIFORNIA! #6**	$4.50
☐	26546	**COLORADO! #7**	$4.50
☐	26069	**NEVADA! #8**	$4.50
☐	26163	**WASHINGTON! #9**	$4.50
☐	26073	**MONTANA! #10**	$4.50
☐	26184	**DAKOTA! #11**	$4.50
☐	26521	**UTAH! #12**	$4.50
☐	26071	**IDAHO! #13**	$4.50
☐	26367	**MISSOURI! #14**	$4.50
☐	27141	**MISSISSIPPI! #15**	$4.50
☐	25247	**LOUISIANA! #16**	$4.50
☐	25622	**TENNESSEE! #17**	$4.50
☐	26022	**ILLINOIS! #18**	$4.50
☐	26533	**WISCONSIN! #19**	$4.50
☐	26849	**KENTUCKY! #20**	$4.50
☐	27065	**ARIZONA! #21**	$4.50
☐	27458	**NEW MEXICO! #22**	$4.50
☐	27703	**OKLAHOMA! #23**	$4.50
☐	28180	**CELEBRATION! #24**	$4.50